The General Retires and Other Stories

NGUYEN HUY THIEP

The General Retires
and Other Stories

Translated from Vietnamese with an Introduction by
GREG LOCKHART

SINGAPORE
OXFORD UNIVERSITY PRESS
OXFORD NEW YORK
1992

Oxford University Press, Walton Street, Oxford OX2 6DP

Oxford New York Toronto
Delhi Bombay Calcutta Madras Karachi
Kuala Lumpur Singapore Hong Kong Tokyo
Nairobi Dar es Salaam Cape Town
Melbourne Auckland Madrid

and associated companies in
Berlin Ibadan

Oxford is a trade mark of Oxford University Press

Published in the United States
by Oxford University Press, New York

© Oxford University Press Pte. Ltd., Singapore, 1992

British Library Cataloguing in Publication Data
Data available

Library of Congress Cataloging-in-Publication Data

Nguyen, Huy Thiep.
[Short stories. English]
The general retires and other stories/Nguyen Huy Thiep; translated from
Vietnamese with an introduction by Greg Lockhart.
p. cm
ISBN 0-19-588580-5 (paper)
1. Short stories, Vietnamese—Translations into English. 2. Short stories,
English—Translations from Vietnamese. I. Title.
PL4378.9.N5168A53 1993
895 92233—dc20
92–14767
CIP

Typeset by Indah Photosetting Centre Sdn. Bhd., Malaysia
Printed by Peter Chong Printers Sdn. Bhd., Malaysia
Published by Oxford University Press Pte. Ltd.,
Unit 221, Ubi Avenue 4, Singapore 1440

Preface

IN September 1988, I had just begun to take an interest in Vietnamese literature at the Australian National University, when an American colleague at Hanoi University, Chris Goscha, sent me a book of collected Vietnamese short stories. The book had been published by the Literature and Art Publishing House in Da Nang earlier that year under the title of one of the stories in it: 'The General Retires', by a writer named Nguyen Huy Thiep. As it turned out, I left the book unread, because I was too busy with my own preparations to depart for Hanoi University which had also offered me the opportunity to work there. But I would come across this title again, when Goscha, finding I had not read the book he sent me, kindly produced another copy soon after I arrived in Hanoi in January 1989.

This was a good time to be there and to receive the second offering. In December 1986, the Vietnamese Communist Party had announced a policy of 'renovation' in all spheres, including literature. With the government wanting to make contacts with 'capitalist' countries, my invitation to study at Hanoi University therefore coincided with an exciting shift in Vietnamese literary thinking. There had been nothing like it since the period of the Popular Front in the late 1930s when temporary freedom of expression permitted by the colonial government produced such major literary figures as Nhat Linh, Xuan Dieu, Ngo

Tat To, and Nam Cao. And, indeed, the literary project of the late 1980s was a clear reaction against the propaganda which many felt had passed for literature in the intervening dark age.

I now saw this reflected in the volume Goscha gave me. I also came to see it reflected in the works of virtually every prominent writer who published between about 1987 and 1990: the playwright Lu Quang Vu, and the novelists and short story writers Nguyen Minh Chau, Le Luu, Nguyen Khai, Nguyen Quang Lap, Duong Thu Huong, Pham Thi Hoai, and Nguyen Huy Thiep. In each case, including N. H. Thiep's, there was a significant departure from the revolutionary romanticism which had dominated Vietnamese literature since the 1940s. But, with N. H. Thiep, many felt that his work focused so directly on the dark age and yet offered such a complex, life-like picture of society that it seemed to stand on its own. As I began to read his stories with fascination and particularly after my first meeting with him on a park bench, I became aware that a number of critics were reaching back to the classics of the 1930s to find some precedent for the quality of his contribution.

Yet my decision to translate N. H. Thiep's work was not only prompted by the sensation his work was causing in Vietnam. Even before I had the opportunity to study in Hanoi, I had long been attuned to the possibility of doing something about the lack of attention to Vietnamese literature beyond its borders. Since I did not begin the translations until long after I had made the decision, I could also have changed it easily, had not my continuing fascination with N. H. Thiep's work been encouraged by the attention it came to attract internationally.

Before I left Hanoi in July 1989, I was aware that a number of French and American journalists had come to interview N. H. Thiep, and that representatives of *éditions de l'aube* in Paris had paid him a visit. The *Far Eastern Economic Review* noted his work by August. A number of reprintings of N. H. Thiep's stories, most notably of 'The General Retires', were beginning to appear in Vietnamese *émigré* journals in Europe, Australia, and Canada. In 1990, Kim Lefèvre's French translation of four of N. H. Thiep's stories were published by *éditions de l'aube* under the title, *Un général à la retraite*. In May that year, I also published an article which contained some information about N. H. Thiep's work in *The Age Monthly Review* in Melbourne. This information was recycled through the *Asian Wall Street Journal* in Hong Kong, from where it was again recycled by a Vietnamese television weekly in Melbourne before I finally read it in Vietnamese. It is indicative of the impact which Vietnamese affairs have had on the world, and vice versa, that N. H. Thiep's new construction of Vietnamese society confirmed my original intuition that Vietnamese literature could not entirely be kept at home.

Among the intellectual and other debts I have incurred while turning eight of N. H. Thiep's stories into English, I should like to make special mention of four. The first of these is to the Vietnamese Faculty at Hanoi University which gave me the opportunity to study Vietnamese literature on its home ground, and the second is to the excellent *Vietnamese Dictionary* published under the general editorship of Hoang Phe by the Social Sciences Publishing House in Hanoi in 1988. Because of its clarity and its comprehensiveness, I found this work an indispensable aid. The third debt I must acknowledge is a personal one to Dr Howard Dick of the University of Newcastle. He not only encouraged my work but also provided the word-processing facilities that were necessary to produce the initial manuscript. The fourth debt I have is the greatest. This is to my wife,

Monique, a native Vietnamese speaker, whose authentic knowledge, intelligent comments, and moral support deepened my contact with the culture it gave me so much interest and pleasure to translate. To her I am most grateful.

Finally, I would like to thank the *Journal of Vietnamese Studies* which published 'Cun' and 'Salt of the Jungle' in January 1991 and *Vietnam Today* which published 'Run River Run' in May 1991 for permission to republish with slight changes these three stories.

Sydney   GREG LOCKHART
February 1992

Contents

Introduction

Nguyen Huy Thiep and
the Faces of Vietnamese Literature

 *One*

NGUYEN HUY THIEP was born in 1950 in French-occupied Hanoi where his mother was a small-goods vendor. Later in the same year, however, she took him to the north-west where he lived in various provinces for the next nine years: Phu Tho, Thai Nguyen, Lang Son, Phuc Yen. During this period, N. H. Thiep's mother turned her hand to agricultural labour and, up to the armistice in 1954, economic hardship and the upheavals caused by the war contributed to the unstable life of the two. In the mid-1950s, the turmoil caused by the Ho Chi Minh government's Maoist land reform campaign exacerbated the instability. But in view of the Christian themes in some of N. H. Thiep's stories— 'Run River Run', 'A Drop of Blood', 'The Water Nymph'—it is notable that, in the midst of the rural upheaval, there was a period when he lived in a church and read the Bible before he was ten.

After moving back to Hanoi in 1960, N. H. Thiep completed his secondary education and studied at the Teachers' College, where he read history. At some point he also read such Chinese classics as *The Three Kingdoms*, and one student of his work has suggested that the cold style of the first century BC Chinese historian, Si Ma Qian, has influenced his writing. Other early literary influences on N. H. Thiep were the nineteenth-century Russian novelists he read in Vietnamese translation. Meanwhile, he graduated from the Teachers' College in 1970, even as American bombs rained down on the country. Humble origins, visions of war, wide reading, high education, and long periods of residence in both remote provinces and the capital had therefore shaped N. H. Thiep's life by the time he was twenty.

After graduating from the Teachers' College, he returned to the north-west, to remote Son La Province where, for ten years, he taught history, wrote, and painted. At one point during the post-1975 exodus from Vietnam, the French journal *Libération* reported in 1990 that N. H. Thiep contemplated leaving the country through Laos, because of the 'primitive' conditions of life in Vietnam. Feeling that he would lose his roots and his power as a writer, however, he finally decided not to go. Instead, he returned once more to Hanoi in 1980, where he worked at various occupations, including acquiring paper and drawing illustrations for various publishing houses. He lived with his wife and children and continued to work on his writing, until he began to publish in major journals in early 1987. But whatever the rate of N. H. Thiep's development as a writer, this timing had an important political dimension.

By late 1986, the political change then sweeping the socialist world had converged with widespread discontent about the standard of living in Vietnam, and forced major Gorbachev-style adjustments to official policy that extended to literature and the arts. In this context, the Vietnamese Communist Party's decision to announce greater literary freedom in December 1986 clearly had a bearing on the timing of N. H. Thiep's first major publication in January 1987: 'The Breezes of Hua Tat', which appeared in the prestigious journal of the National Writers' Association, *Literature and Art*.

From this point, *Literature and Art* added popularity to its prestige, as it continued to publish N. H. Thiep's work for the next two years. 'The General Retires' attracted widespread attention when it was published in June 1987, because of its unusually stark construction of Vietnamese society. 'Salt of the Jungle' was published in July, and 'A Drop of Blood' and 'The Water Nymph' maintained the interest of many readers, before it was intensified by the storm which erupted in the political–literary bureaucracy over the publication of three historical stories in the first half of 1988. These were 'Fired Gold', 'A Sharp Sword', and 'Chastity' which gave important Vietnamese historical figures unusual and unflattering fictional lives.

In late 1988, a collected edition of N. H. Thiep's works was then presented to the public by Youth Publishing House in Ho Chi Minh City. Six months later Culture Publishing House in Hanoi produced a second collected edition, and the Hue literary journal, *Perfume River*, published 'Cun' separately. By this time, some twenty of N. H. Thiep's stories had generated over ninety critical articles in major journals alone, and 1988 was being widely referred to as the year of the 'Nguyen Huy Thiep phenomenon'. Moreover, with the release of the film version of 'The General Retires' in early 1989, the intense interest even spread to the Hanoi High Command.

On 18 February 1989, the *People's Army Daily* reported that N. H. Thiep's film had been the subject of a questionnaire which asked political cadres, technical cadres, senior colonels, and generals to comment on various aspects of the film, including some bizarre touches that will be mentioned later. The results of the questionnaire were complex, although certain trends were clear: technical cadres were most likely to praise the film, as some 40 per cent did; political cadres and generals were most likely to disapprove strongly, as some 60 per cent in each category did. In any case, the questionnaire reflected both the seriousness with which literature is taken in Vietnamese society and the impact of N. H. Thiep's work. By 1990, apart from the short stories and the film script, N. H. Thiep had written another two plays and a critical essay.

Meanwhile, the year 1990 was an important one for the renovation project. This was the time when the authorities, fearing the course of change in the Soviet Union and Eastern Europe, began significantly to dampen the freedom of expression which had given Vietnamese literature a new lease of life. Journalists were given political directions about how to report the decline of the Communist Party in the Soviet Union. The works of the most prominent writers, including N. H. Thiep, also began to disappear from bookshops, and their names became taboo.

The situation is likely to fluctuate in the future. Literary revivals and mini-revivals punctuated by strong bouts of official disapproval are quite possible, as the Vietnamese government espouses economic development and grapples with its fears of freedom and change. However, the sequence of sudden appearance and shadowy disappearance of the renovation literature confirms that N. H. Thiep's stories are inscriptions of a culture where politics and literature are intimately related. They are best understood, therefore, in relation to a particular political–literary agenda: the renovation agenda, out of which, as well as against the backdrop of which, their originality comes into view.

Two

The renovation agenda stemmed from a perception that, in the mindless wartime propagation of socialist realism, the quality of Vietnamese literature had seriously declined. The war novelist, Nguyen Minh Chau, thus said as early as 1979 that the literature was dominated by what he described as a kind of wishful thinking 'doctrinaire-ism' (*chu nghia phai dao*), and others developed this point. For example, the literary critic, Professor Hoang Ngoc Hien, argued in a seminal article how, in their 'description of life the way others want it to be', Vietnamese writers produced work that bore little relation to reality. What had emerged was a kind of chronic 'information aesthetics' (*thong tin my thuat*) or thinly disguised state propaganda. Herein, 'vague and insipid characters' with 'uniform characteristics' were detached from history and marshalled in 'simple, even crude' narratives according to some official dream of revolutionary heroism (Hoang Ngoc Hien, 1979). However, with wars against China and Kampuchea in full swing on all fronts, 1979 was not a good year for an anti-heroic critique. And although a number of muted voices continued to support such a critique through the first half of the 1980s it was not until the sea change in Communist Party policy from 1986 that it began to have a sweeping effect on literary production.

In this context, the aptness of the metaphor of a 'sea change' in Communist Party policy is worth stressing, because it is dictated by basic assumptions about the nature of the political–literary process. In fact, in Vietnam, where the term for 'culture' itself, *van hoa*, may be translated literally into English as 'the change which literature (and art) brings about', literary production takes place in an environment where its capacity to intervene in the political process is widely assumed. A shadow line between politics and literature thus parallels the autocratic nature of government. This does not necessarily mean that the government attempts crudely to impose a line. Generally it attempts to 'manage' (*quan ly*) a consensus through discussions in the national literary bodies. Nevertheless, a failure of 'management' can result in rough-house tactics. The sacking of editors and the closure of publishing houses is always possible. Given the special tensions which are involved in creative literary production in Vietnam, therefore, pressure for ideological change can build up in the political cross-currents for a long time and, when the situation is right, suddenly surge through the bureaucracy.

This is what happened by 1987, and an influential essay which the critic Dr Le Ngoc Tra published in 1988 conveys a good sense of the specific issues which flooded the renovation agenda around this time. One of the essay's main points was an attack on the way revolutionary heroism was bound to the traditional 'epic' (*su thi*) form:

For many years now, our literature has had the task of building up an image of HISTORY, THE COUNTRY OF OUR AN-CESTORS, THE PEOPLE, THE MASSES. But we are too absorbed in the 'epic' form, in the collective image of people, and pay too little attention to the task of describing the destinies of people and establishing original images of individual persons and their lives. THE PERSON is usually only described by a few simple outlines sketched into a general picture of the glorious mass of the people. One of the demands made of works about war and revolution has required that writers describe the destiny of people in the whirlwind of history. Therefore, literature only reflects the person through its descriptions of history, but it needs to reflect history through descriptions of the destiny of the person (Le Ngoc Tra, 1990, pp. 45–6). [Capitals in the original.]

Brimming here at the crest of the anti-heroic critique initiated in the late 1970s is, then, the sea change. 'History', the global category which comprehends the changing lives and fortunes of people in society, is overpowered in the cross-currents by 'person', the individual subjectivity which lives history. In a number of the most acclaimed works of the renovation period, the revolutionary hero was therefore displaced rapidly by the individual in whose suffering person history was now concentrated and absorbed.

One reviewer of Le Luu's new wave war novel, *Thoi xa vang* [The Old Days] (1987), thought it admirable that this clear account of the struggle of the peasant soldier, Sai, against feudalism and imperialism and, also, against anachronistic family obligations contained 'no heroes' (Hoang Ngoc Hien, 1987). Pham Thi Hoai set her savage novel, *Thien Su* [The Crystal Messenger] (1988), around the deeply pessimistic outlook of an ugly duckling character—also named Hoai—whose thirst for love and affection dominated the story. Duong Thu Huong and Nguyen Huy Thiep were other major writers whose works attacked the heroic illusion. But, before showing how they did, it is important to stress that sea changes do not empty the ocean; they reveal new aspects of it. Despite the change of image, the renovation agenda was still politically prescribed.

The sacking of Nguyen Ngoc, the editor of *Literature and Art*, in December 1988 demonstrated this. The sacking was carried out on the basis of an 'administrative decision' of the Executive of the National Writers' Association, which it never satisfactorily explained. Nevertheless, it was widely believed that Nguyen Ngoc's problem was generally related to his publication of N. H. Thiep's work, and particularly related to his publication of 'Chastity'—the historical story in which N. H. Thiep suggests that Nguyen Hue, the eighteenth-century culture hero who defeated a Chinese army of invasion, had a lascivious passion for beautiful girls.

Even *Swallow's Wing*, a small journal published by the

Phu Khanh Literature and Art Association, could produce evidence in April 1989 which aligned the editor's demise with a comment made by one of the executive members of the Writers' Association. As *Swallow's Wing* reported, the executive member had exclaimed: 'If we denigrate Nguyen Hue today, tomorrow we will denigrate Uncle Ho' (p. 15). The limitations of the renovation agenda were clear: the present was to be preserved in a pristine past and, in this backward-looking vision, a questioning of the historical foundations and political morality of the state was not possible.

By the time of Nguyen Ngoc's sacking, however, many of the major renovation works had been written along lines which suggest that the writers already sensed the limits of the agenda, even as they tested them. On the one hand, 'renovation' did not imply permission to write direct criticism of the superstructure of the state. On the other hand, with considerable support for administrative and economic reforms emanating from the government, it did imply scope to pull down corrupt façades in the refurbishing of the political–moral order. The difficulty here, of course, was that, with great poverty and dissatisfaction in Vietnam, the tearing down of façades could reveal new faces of the problem and open up vistas which the government found disturbing. But, while Nguyen Ngoc's shabby treatment was only a precursor to the dampening of the project in 1990, a preoccupation with faces and façades was, by definition, central to the agenda of the *renovation* writers.

Lu Quang Vu's popular, satirical play of 1988 about the grandiose schemes and useless projects of a commune chief clearly dealt with questions of face. Given the new accent on the person, the private face of the individual also gave the major writers new territory to explore. For example, in her novel, *Chuyen tinh ke truoc luc rang dong* [Love Stories

Told before Dawn] (1988), Duong Thu Huong provided intimate, suffering portraits of her main characters as she explored the Party's intervention in the private lives of people. In *Nhung thien duong mu* [Blind Paradises] (1988) her fiction revealed similar inclinations, as it dealt with the effects of the mid-1950s land reform campaign on the lives of individuals. Perhaps one senses that the political edge of such works prefigured Duong Thu Huong's own destiny: she was expelled from the Communist Party in 1990 and imprisoned for several months on spurious charges in 1991. But, still, her novel, *Cac vi nhan tinh le* [Big Men in Little Provinces] (1988), opened with an attack on rotten façades that fell well within what might be described as the standard renovation agenda.

The very first paragraph focuses on some glass-fronted display cabinets in a muddy provincial coffee-shop. Flies are buzzing around the cabinets and, having found a way to slip inside, are crawling all over the moon cakes and pastries that are dry and stiff. Meanwhile, at the counter, '... the girl in charge yawns without trying to hide two rows of rotten teeth.' This striking blemish also lies behind the smile of one of N. H. Thiep's characters in 'A Drop of Blood' such that it begins to acquire the status of a cliché. However, the attention which N. H. Thiep gives to faces is also notable for its deep roots in Vietnamese culture. In 'The Water Nymph', for example, the peasant youth, Chuong, dreams of the faces of people he knows. But with some as pale as a 'buffalo's scrotum' and others with the 'jaw bones of a horse', he sees 'no human faces among them, just animal faces' that are wrinkled with suffering and filled with shame.

This identification of people with animals, which, incidentally, has been common in Vietnamese literature for centuries, is also at work in N. H. Thiep's other stories. It is, for example, very explicit in 'Salt of the Jungle', where murky inklings of animal–human affinities are aroused in an extraordinary tale that includes vivid description of the face of a monkey. But, since we are now in the realm of the animal-human, there is one remarkable case of some faces— or is it one face?—in the renovation literature which further illustrates the depth and intensity of the cultural response that was possible within the prescription.

This example appears in Nguyen Minh Chau's fifty-page story, 'Phien Cho Giat' [Time of Giat Market] which he completed on his deathbed in 1988. The story tells much about an old peasant's feelings for his son who has recently been killed in the war in Kampuchea, and for the buffalo his poverty is now forcing him to sell at the market for slaughter. Here is the opening paragraph:

Old Khung woke up. He woke up suddenly, because of a terrifying dream. In his feverish sleep, he saw the figure of a very tall, bony old man with strands of short hair, stiff like bamboo shoots, bristling on the right side of his head and spiking his forehead in a mixture of black and white; his face and nose were rough, his eyes staring; bull's blood smeared the muscles of his shoulders and upper arms in streaks, some wet, some dry, as he lifted with both arms above his head a sledgehammer—as heavy as the one used by the blacksmith's assistant at the furnace at the head of Khoi Village—and smashed it down into the middle of the bull's head, so that the sledgehammer blow struck the bull's forehead between the eyes, causing one of them to drop out of its socket in a stream of blood (Nguyen Minh Chau, 1989, p. 124).

Note the faces. The first one is not distinct. It appears fleetingly in nine words as nothing more than a rough surface with a nose which recedes, around its staring eyes, into a terrifying vision of hair, muscle, blood, and bone. Meanwhile, the face of the bull, outlined only by the line of the 'forehead between the eyes', disintegrates into instant nothingness under the impact of the hammer blow. With

old Khung's face, the unwritten mirror image, we are looking at composite animal–human faces emptied by the vi-
olence into which they disappear.

This is the horror of the dark age. It is the horror of what
Pham Thi Hoai, in her very different but still major
treatment of 'faces' in *Thien su* [The Crystal Messenger],
suggests is the 'dispersal' of people, to the point where they
have become 'faceless'. Pham Thi Hoai's faceless ones are
caught in a series of seventeen short chapters—twenty in the
French edition—which play explicitly on the simile of the
swivelling surfaces of a 'rubic cube'. Because of the blank-
ness of this image, her treatment of facelessness might not be
as directly evocative of war and rural poverty as Nguyen
Minh Chau's. Nor, perhaps, does it have the immediate
impact of N. H. Thiep's account of the face of the severed
head in 'Run River Run'. Her vision is, in some ways, a
colder, even more frightening one of political–social extinc-
tion. But visions of both war and repression appear with
varying degrees of intensity and explicit description on the
faces which were created by the most prominent writers of
the late 1980s.

A concern to reveal the face, or the facelessness, of the
person was central to their agenda, because, within the
limits of renovation, the construction of new faces (and
façades) was essential for the creation of a more perfect
political–moral order. However, the great fascination and
importance of N. H. Thiep's stories is that although the
anti-heroic emphasis of the period conditioned their concerns, it neither limited nor constructed them.
N. H. Thiep's stories do not simply displace one image by
another. They create complex *multifaceted* images that cut
across the usual boundaries. In this they are like Pham Thi
Hoai's 'rubic cube'. Yet this simile does not really suggest
the deep roots which N. H. Thiep's stories have in

Vietnamese culture, for it is by presenting the old faces of Vietnam in a complex new way that N. H. Thiep's writing reveals an exceptional capacity to override the central disjunction of the standard renovation agenda.

_____ *Three* _____

In Vietnam, the idea of a person with an individual identity is clearly 'modern', in that, in a philosophical sense, it implies a break with historical traditions. In fact, the 'individual' (*ca nhan*) only begins to flicker in Vietnamese literature in the early part of this century, when the Vietnamese term for 'modern' (*can dai*), as opposed to 'new' (*tan*), was itself initially constructed to take account of the unprecedented technological change of the colonial period. Yet the disjunction, which runs all the way through 'modern' Vietnamese literature, recurs in the renovation agenda when its political–moral limits resist any break with history which, if successful, must then embalm the face of the person.

N. H. Thiep is acutely aware of this. Along with his animal–human faces, he gives us the 'impenetrable appearance' of a number of characters such as the monk at Thien Tru Pagoda in 'A Drop of Blood'. Towards the end of the same story, we also have a description of the façade of the Pham family's ancestral house which is slowly crumbling at the head of the stagnant village of Ke Noi, but essentially still the same as it was a hundred years before. What it symbolizes is the history of the family, which has just been recycled through successive generations. These rise to positions of wealth and feudal power and, finally, fall through dissipation to the ground of their peasant origins. But what is so striking about the main characters in the story—the powerful mandarins, Pham Ngoc Chieu and Pham Ngoc Phong—is that their appearances are not impenetrable.

We learn, for example, that the heroic reputation Chieu has gained for fighting the French is entirely misplaced. The reputation initially spread after Chieu had a French missionary thrashed and was dismissed from his post by the Imperial Court. People said that Chieu had set himself apart from the foreign invaders and the corrupt court. As it happened, however, Chieu did not know that the missionary had influential friends at court when, in his vanity and arrogance, he thrashed him for daring to pass the front of his District Office in a sedan chair without stopping to pay his respects. By playing the illusion off against many dark aspects of Chieu's career, N. H. Thiep thus does something more complex than most other renovation writers who simply displace the hero image and reveal that of the suffering person. He actually confronts the illusion and presents facets of a life which are not normally revealed.

Moreover, as vile as Chieu may be, he is not entirely evil. Nor is his son, Phong, who is capable of rape and murder. The feudal system their careers perpetuate is also shown to shape their behaviour which can sometimes be loyal and generous. Complex individuals therefore stand out in history and also mark a break from it, because the perspective from which they appear must be outside the feudal history which the story recycles. In 'A Drop of Blood', Thiep's complex individuals are constructed *across* a temporal break, such that the recycling of history is not a latent structural property of the story. It is its deep subject.

The conscious play on the disjunction between history and the break with history then produces its dramatic tension. A similar play on various temporal and spatial breaks also produces the complex characters and dramatic tensions in many of N. H. Thiep's other stories. In 'Run River Run', for example, we have a dramatization of some elemental cleavage in the order of the universe. In the early part of the story, a young boy's dreams of miracles along a stretch of river are offset by the brutal world of the hungry fishermen who cast their nets along it each night. Later, the boy leaves the river. He moves to the city, grows up, and forgets his dreams. But on a chance return visit to the river many years later, a sad encounter reminds him both of his childhood dreams and the harsh world they did not change. In their futility, the importance of the dreams is, finally, that their memory intensifies his sadness at the darkness of the world and the river's endless flow.

'Cun', the story of the deformed beggar, is a good example of how fertile as well as futile the tensions in a story can be. We know from almost the beginning that Cun is about to die. But we soon learn that during his miserable, short life he had what by the standards of the renovation literature was an unexpected asset: an 'unusually beautiful face'. As this face illuminates his gross deformities, it makes people so doubly 'uneasy' that they shower him with money, which is in turn linked to the miraculous birth of his son, a moment before he dies 'blissfully' in the mud. Here the disjunction is between life and death. Yet, in a characteristic N. H. Thiep strategy, it doubles the one between the history that dooms Cun from the beginning and the break with history, marked by the bliss. Precisely because Cun is doomed from the beginning, his beautiful face heightens the tension in the story which produces unexpected facets of life—the baby—that are free-floating and can never be taken for granted.

In 'Lessons from the Country', we can also float free. A naïve city boy, Hieu, goes on a holiday in the country. Events, such as an incipient, but unfulfilled, romance between Hieu and Hien, a girl he meets, set up complex tensions across the separation between country and city, the spatial analogues of the old and new. On the one hand, Hieu's naïvety opens our eyes to peasant virtues and what is sometimes the awesome beauty of country landscapes and girls. On the other hand, even as it transports us, this beauty heightens our awareness of what lies in the shadows of country life: danger, boredom, and a rapacious urban élite. Rising above such tensions and floating free, however, the beautiful kite flying passage suggests release and another detached point of view. As it soars high above the confused wind currents that imperil it close to the ground, the kite tilts its face at the earth, first in 'disdain' and then in a 'salute'.

The perspective of the kite thus poses a general question: how are we to understand the heightened, free-floating point of view from which so many complex facets of life are perceived? The answer to these questions begins, I think, with a *way of writing*, which could not be further from the oral tradition in which a story is related in successive, transparent retellings that establish the layers of its moral authority. And Professor Hoang Ngoc Hien, who helped to initiate the renovation debate in 1979, came close to saying this in a paper he delivered at the Hanoi Teacher's College in 1988.

What Professor Hien observed on this occasion was that whereas almost all Vietnamese writers 'relate' or 'narrate the content' of their stories (*ke lai noi dung*), N. H. Thiep, along with perhaps only Nguyen Khai and Pham Thi Hoai, 'writes the content' (*viet noi dung*) of his. In Professor Hien's formulation, those who 'relate content' only pay attention 'to a task: that of relating something', while those who 'write content' also pay attention to 'how to relate it'. But what does this mean? Professor Hien suggested it means that those who relate stories simply use prose to 'carry news' of some important tidings. They are little concerned with the creation of tone and tension in a work, such that they offer little sense of the different points of view one finds in the work of those who 'write content'. However, what is crucial here is that, unlike the 'writers', the 'relaters' are still close to the oral tradition which assumes that language is transparent.

Duong Thu Huong's novels are a good example of this position. In their accounts of the suffering individual, they bring news of official stupidity and corruption. They are informed by a fiery renovation vision, and assume that words are clear windows on reality, through which meaning and authority can be recovered from some anterior source. On the other hand, as N. H. Thiep's multiple points of view suggest, his narrative does not rest on such assumptions. What we are dealing with in his case is a very different preoccupation with language and writing itself, which, as a temporal sequence of signs, produces what Derrida teaches us is a continual deferral of meaning. By placing the accent on time, this deferral permits the narrative to float free of the political–moral authority which sets up the temporal disjunction of the renovation agenda. By placing the accent on shifting points of view, it also reveals individual differences between people which have the same effect.

Hence, the euphoria of those many readers who felt that their imaginations were being set free in a new way of viewing society. Hence, also, the disturbance of the conservative critics who nevertheless read on with fascination and horror. What these critics singled out for most attention, of course, were the bizarre details of cruelty, hunger, and lust which figure in the stories. In a typical conservative explanation of this dark side of N. H. Thiep's writing, the critic, Mai Ngu, thus suggested something cold, irresponsible, even 'pathological' (Tap chi, 1990, p. 161) in the nature of the writer. Yet such an explanation does justice to neither the depth and sensitivity of N. H. Thiep's stories nor the skill of a gifted artist whose work gripped even its fiercest critics. Mai Ngu also said, 'I do not hide that I like a few of his stories, and among those "The Water Nymph"' (Tap chi, 1990, p. 161). Furthermore, Mai Ngu made another comment in the same essay which may have hinted that he was himself aware of the limitations of his explanation.

In this comment Mai Ngu makes a reference to the 'sharp, differentiating pen' which N. H. Thiep turns on 'each person', and uses to 'saw through the heart of the reader' (Tap chi, 1990, p. 159). What is interesting about this reference is that, although it is meant to indicate N. H. Thiep's heartlessness, it still conveys an inkling that the bizarre details are not what is fundamentally at stake. Indeed, it is most reasonable to argue that N. H. Thiep's pen seems so 'sharp', *because*, in its deferral of meaning, it is writing a new narrative of *differences* between people which cuts—or 'saws'—across a temporal break and thereby accentuates our sense of a society being trapped in the past. This entrapment then produces the bizarre details, as well as all the others.

'The General Retires' may be taken to illustrate this point. In this story an old general returns to his son's house on the outskirts of Hanoi after a long life of devoted service to the country. In the early part of the story, Thuan, the general's son, who is also the narrator, describes his relationship with his wife, Thuy, in the following terms:

the relationship between my wife and me is amicable. Thuy is well educated and lives the life of a modern woman. We each have our way of thinking.... Thuy is as well in control of the family economy as she is of the children's education. As for me, it seems that I'm old-fashioned, awkward and full of contradictions.

Now, there are three points to make about this typical passage. First, its spare, short sentences were singled out by some Vietnamese critics who said they lacked 'art' that was commensurate with Vietnamese literature. Second, it is clearly structured by individual differences through which the characters, though in an amicable relationship and belonging together, stand out in sharp relief against each other. One is old-fashioned, the other modern, and both have different ways of thinking. Thus, third, we have a new way of writing in Vietnam that depends on differences to construct characters across a disjunction between the old-fashioned and the modern.

Both Thuan, an engineer, and Thuy, a doctor, emerge as ambiguous characters. Thuan is passive, but not necessarily weak. Even though Thuy objects strongly to the confusion caused by the stream of visitors coming to the house to welcome the general home, he still has a pig slaughtered and invites everyone in the village to join the celebrations in accordance with ancient custom. 'Although my village is near the city,' he says, 'the customs of the countryside are still very strong.' Thuan's passive acceptance of such customs reflects their strength. It also reflects the social backdrop against which the behaviour of a 'modern' woman like Thuy can stand out in bizarre and ambiguous ways.

These are reflected in many details. But none is more arresting than the description of Thuy's scheme to bring aborted foetuses home from a maternity clinic to feed a pack of Alsatians she is raising to make money. This touch is open to various interpretations, including the remarkable banality of Thuy's behaviour. But another interpretation is that her behaviour is perfectly reasonable. Good guard dogs are in demand among Hanoi householders for security purposes, and, as many Vietnamese read the story, Thuy does have to keep a household going in a moral void where illu-

sions about socialist cost accounting sink into the general-
ized poverty which reduces life to its material foundations.
When the general points out what Thuy has been doing,
Thuan simply says: 'I had in fact known about this, but
overlooked it as something of no importance.'

At the climax of the story, where the general is driven
away from family and society because of the emptiness he
finds there, the implications are far-reaching: the general is
disheartened not so much by his daughter-in-law's ruthless
behaviour as by his realization that such behaviour is com-
monplace in contemporary society. This searing observation
is nevertheless tempered by the author's ambivalent characterization of Thuy. As a good deal of dialogue shows, Thuy
is not necessarily insensitive to other people's feelings, and
her behaviour is, in the final analysis, more hard-headed
than hard-hearted. Thus cutting across the old-fashioned
and the modern, N. H. Thiep's perspective of individual
differences produced a 'sharp' story that many Vietnamese
readers felt was a devastating social commentary.

One other example of the interplay of individual differences may be related to a particular aspect of N. H. Thiep's
work which has received considerable attention: its construction of woman characters. One Western scholar has
argued, for example, that the characterization of Thuy in
'The General Retires' is a masculine construction (White,
1989). In most of N. H. Thiep's stories, women also appear
variously in what Western feminists might describe as classic
male roles of schemer, temptress, mother, saviour, victim.
Meanwhile, there are two main Vietnamese ways of stating
the problem. One way is to argue that N. H. Thiep's construction of women disdains the fairer sex; the other way is
to argue the reverse, as Professor Hien most notably does.
According to him, N. H. Thiep's construction of women
highlights the importance of the 'feminine principle' (*nguyen*

tac tinh nu) in the world and its emphasis on the idea of salvation through beauty, sweetness, and light (Tap chi, 1990, pp. 109–11, 191). However, a problem with all these arguments—Western feminist and Vietnamese—is that they suggest that N. H. Thiep's women characters represent a single ideological centre.

One writer who implicitly recognizes this problem is Tran Thanh Dam. In an essay which offers a critique of Professor Hien's application of the 'feminine principle' to N. H. Thiep's stories, he points out that while many women characters in the stories suggest commendable models for human behaviour, there are many others including Thieu Hoa in 'A Drop of Blood' who 'come to nothing' (Tap chi, 1990, p. 191). Also, there are admirable men characters in the stories such as the retired general. Drawing on the ancient classics, Tran Thanh Dam further points out that, in any case, there is nothing new about the idea of the 'feminine principle'. Because the *Book of Changes* did 'not divide female nature from male nature' (Tap chi, 1990, p. 192), many ancient writers with an eye for beautiful women had a conception which permitted them to illuminate the whole world with a dazzling feminine radiance. The classical origin of this radiance in N. H. Thiep's stories thus becomes apparent, especially when they assume no basic divide between male and female nature. A feminine radiance shines from Cun's 'unusually beautiful face', and in 'Lessons from the Country', another may even be seen to suffuse the landscape with its awesome glow. But even though it alerts us to the classical influences at work in N. H. Thiep's stories, Tran Thanh Dam's essay does not attempt to build these influences into a single ideological centre. In fact, the essay suggests the full complexity of the situation in which N. H. Thiep's play on modern individual differences between people greatly complicates, but does not necessarily contradict, a classical attachment to the 'feminine principle'.

In addition to discussing the 'feminine principle', Tran Thanh Dam's essay questions Professor Hien's application of the classical virtues of 'heart' (*tam*) and 'benevolence' (*long nhan ai*) to N. H. Thiep's work. What is at issue here is the debate which N. H. Thiep's stark realism has caused about the meaning of 'humanism' and, in particular, the kind of humanism which will best serve the individual, whether masculine or feminine, and the society in modern Vietnam. Within this debate, Professor Hien has tended to accommodate the old ideas of 'heart' and 'benevolence' to modern ideas of the individual. If N. H. Thiep's characters 'saw through the heart of the reader', as Mai Ngu puts it, Professor Hien would argue that this is because of the author's humanist concern to depict the shame and suffering which an unjust world inflicts on individuals. For his part, Tran Thanh Dam does not necessarily see the virtue in this argument. He draws attention to the kind of 'cynical humanism' (Tap chi, 1990, p. 198) which such an approach can encourage. His tendency, therefore, is to accommodate humanism to the old values in which the good heart and benevolent attitude of a writer are inconsistent with shocking his readers. Despite this classical reaction, however, Tran Thanh Dam does not ignore the need to deal with the modern individual. He is still conscious of the necessity to integrate old and new values, and, although he does not clarify the method of integration, it is this consciousness which implicitly allows him to relate the 'feminine principle' to modern concerns about humanism that go beyond the question of women.

Along with 'heart' and 'benevolence', the 'feminine principle' is, indeed, one of the 'elements' of 'humanism in literature', as Tran Thanh Dam finally alludes to it. Put another way, the question of women becomes an aspect of 'humanism', of the problem of the 'individual personality', and of the conflict 'between the individual and the community, the "I" and the "we"' (Tap chi, 1990, p. 199). In a society where it is by no means certain that human beings have 'human rights', the question of women must therefore be posed most plausibly as an aspect of fundamental questions which modernity has raised about the freedom and dignity of human beings in general. Moreover, the breadth and the depth of the debate which N. H. Thiep's women characters arouse certainly makes it fitting that he has constructed them in the same way as he has constructed his men ones: by manifesting their complex differences and thus breaking down any idea of a single centre.

Thuy's strong role in 'The General Retires' is too complex to be simply a masculine construct. In 'A Mother's Soul', the strong figure of the girl–mother, Thu, appears in an explicit interplay of the 'different' family backgrounds and feelings which establish her relationship with Dang, the orphan boy. In 'Lessons From the Country', the passage about Hien's boredom and frustration in the country actually amounts to a questioning of the inequalities between the sexes which it consciously describes. Here we find her saying: '. . . women are worth nothing. But there are many men who aren't worth much either.' In 'A Drop of Blood' some of N. H. Thiep's women characters can be vile and meretricious, but they can also be victims. What is of greatest interest in this story, however, is the way the individuality of Dieu, Hue Lien, and Chiem emerges, as N. H. Thiep applies the most ruthless realism to set their lives in the patriarchal and polygamous feudal order, and then dooms them so inexorably that their suffering humanity cries out against the social order and the double standards of men. In the end, the individuality of these women is a comment on the power structure which represses it.

So, to clarify the way N. H. Thiep's stories override the temporal and spatial disjunctions of the standard renovation agenda, one can say that in their deferral of meaning they do not have a single ideological centre; they have multiple centres—Christianity, humanism, socialism, feudalism, democracy, or whatever—that are being constantly constructed and reconstructed by individual differences. Stated in a different way, there is an absence of a single ideological centre in N. H. Thiep's writing, which has a number of important implications.

One, of course, is that no individual has necessarily to appear in a consistent way, and this produces the possibility of something that is alien to the standard renovation agenda: the multiple faces of the same person—bizarre, beautiful, and banal. Another implication is the freedom which the narrative has to release characters from all corners and levels of society's imagination—Cun comes from a drain-pipe, Pham Ngoc Phong from a wealthy estate—into a panorama of Vietnamese life, including the spirit world, that is most impressive in its scope and richness. Yet another implication is the complexity of N. H. Thiep's succinct prose. What some describe as the 'absolute realism' of 'The General Retires' offers no guarantee against the social realism, surrealism, or magical realism that can be found in many stories where myth and history merge. In 'The Water Nymph', for instance, a strong element of social realism is used to detail the back-breaking labour and conflict of life in a peasant community. But it frequently gives way to surreal dream sequences and descriptions of the fields, while ethereal riverscapes capture the mythical element in the story and let it play in the light of the moon.

In all of this, however, the most profound implication of the absence of an ideological centre is that N. H. Thiep does not produce transparent prose. Rather, he produces a narrative whose arbitrary nature fissures the old political–moral ontology, and finally rejects history or translates it into a repository of free-floating signs. In other words, N. H. Thiep's writing marks the possibility of a fundamental shift in literature's position in the culture.

In terms of the way N. H. Thiep's writing marks this shift, it is helpful to know that some aspects of his work are not entirely unprecedented. Although they sought to unify the ideological thrust of their narratives and certainly 're-lated' them, many writers in the 1920s and 1930s had to deal more or less ambiguously with more than one ideological centre. This was inevitable at a time when the literary agenda raised the complex issue of modernization within the context of foreign political domination. One can find modern ideologies at play on pre-modern ones and vice versa in an early Vietnamese novel such as Hoang Ngoc Phach's ambiguous *To tam* [Pure Heart] (1925), for example. In addition, during the 1950s and 1960s, when American domination did not provide an appealing political focus for most southern writers, the ideological content of their work was generally diffuse. And even in the north, where the main literary project since 1945 has been the reconstruction of a single ideological centre under the banner of the Communist Party, there is at least one major example of deconstruction before we get to N. H. Thiep and Pham Thi Hoai: Nguyen Khai's very interesting 1979 novel, *Cha va con va . . .* [Father and Child and . . .], about a young priest who goes into a parish after the revolution.

This work was written at a time of widespread disillusionment with an ideology that seemed only to offer further struggle and to demand more discipline and repression, and its complex narrative encompasses a strong element of ambiguity. When the priest arrives in the parish, for example, the welcome he receives from the local committee is correct but forced, and its format reflects what Nguyen Khai describes as the complex 'colours of the monarchical system in the bosom of a democratic society' (p. 23). A related passage on the next page, in which Nguyen Khai explicitly discusses old honorific forms of address and, there-by, accentuates the complex sense of how values have both changed and remained unchanged, also highlights the assumption that language is not transparent. There is thus a shift in political consciousness—marked by 1979 when the renovation agenda was first mooted—which acknowledges that the democratic revolution has only been a partial success.

By the time we get to N. H. Thiep's work a decade later, however, our sense of this shift comes in on an altogether new level of complexity. Part of the reason for this lies in the different natures of the two writers, because the struc-ture of Nguyen Khai's writing in the late 1980s is not markedly more complex than it was in the late 1970s. It may also be that, unlike Nguyen Khai, an older writer, N. H. Thiep began publishing at a time of unusual freedom of expression. But, even so, there is no doubt that the renovation freedoms were encouraged by a widespread desire for economic development that, by the late 1980s, had a particular edge. This was the edge of post-Vietnam War consumerism. And its great importance here is that, as it sharply focused the desire for political and economic free-doms, it played on the individual differences between people which 'de-centre' N. H. Thiep's narrative and, also, detach it from history to an exceptional extent.

In Vietnam, the onset of new types of consumption, the

rapid rhythm of fashion changes, the intrusion of advertising, and the omnipresence of the international media cannot be compared with those in Western societies or in the advanced Asian ones. Nevertheless, large quantities of American consumer items were introduced during the war and left after it. Aid packages from socialist countries have been considerable. The spread of television has occurred in the cities. Press reporting and advertising have become more diversified. A steady stream of French wines, whisky, watches, videos, motor cycles, and, sometimes, even toilet paper have come from Thailand, Hong Kong, and China. By the late 1980s, downtown Ho Chi Minh City was also showing some signs of a revival of international trade. Against a backdrop of economic underdevelopment and common poverty, therefore, the consumer influx has been sufficient to do two important things: first, highlight the government's own ineffective economic performance; and second, set up new expectations that are not only based on individual consumer differences, but also impossible to satisfy with worn-out political slogans based on tradition and history.

What we are dealing with in Vietnam is not exactly consumerism, but traces of consumerism and consumer frustration which N. H. Thiep uses in his stories to sharpen the outline of the individual in a social context of largely undifferentiated, grinding poverty. In 'The General Retires', for instance, we have Thuan's distinctive taste for Galang cigarettes. These are an expensive Indian brand imported from the Soviet Union which, alas, he has to give up to defray family expenses. In the same story, an inadequate supply of filter cigarettes and a medley of worn-out songs from the Beatles and Abba feature at the wedding feast to play on the (frustrated) bourgeois pretensions of its organizers.

At Pham Ngoc Phong's fiftieth birthday party in 'A Drop of Blood', some French cakes are consumed which actually have Phong's name inscribed on them in butter. However, Phong's individualism is placed in perspective when the village notables, who have been invited to the party, pinch the cake into their mouths and then smear their greasy fingers all over the mats on which they sit. In 'The Water Nymph', the image of the pretty schoolteacher, Phuong, could not highlight more cruelly the narrow horizons and clumsy frustration of the peasant youth, Chuong, who falls in love with her. She has been overseas and, in her remoteness from Chuong, dresses in jeans and a blouse and carries a bag that makes her look like a 'movie actress'. Cigarettes, foreign food, stylish modern clothing, watches, jewellery, and sun-glasses stand out sharply against a dark backdrop of deprivation in N. H. Thiep's stories, and outline the individuality of their consumers with the traces of some imagined bliss.

These, then, are the consumer traces which bring us back to the question about how we are to understand the heightened, free-floating point of view from which N. H. Thiep's stories are perceived. On the one hand, these traces outline vividly the idea of the individual in a society where the desire for modern consumer goods is strong. On the other hand, they create individual outlines of such vividness that they mark the general drabness and poverty of a society in which pre-modern modes of consumption remain entrenched. N. H. Thiep's point of view must therefore be inside society for the individual differences and desires of his characters to come into play, but it must be outside society for this play to develop. In other words, N. H. Thiep's point of view is located in a discourse about modernity which, in a society with a pre-modern economy, has been stimulated by external factors. The consumer traces have come from outside Vietnam and aroused the consumer imagination inside Vietnam, which then hovers high above the society's lack of economic development.

In this reflexive sense, N. H. Thiep's stories work like the kite in 'Lessons from the Country'. In the same way as the kite hovers over the earth to which it is nevertheless tethered by a rattan cord, the heightened point of view in the stories is tethered to society by a string of consumer traces. Like the kite which tilts its face at the earth first in disdain and then in a salute, the stories tilt at a world whose alternatives, contradictions, and differences they dramatize in the split vision which occurs when a largely pre-modern society is viewed from a modern (consumer) perspective. This vision is what detaches the narrative from the time of history, even as the subjects of the narrative remain trapped in the past. It is what sets up the point of view outside history which enables the author to delineate so sharply and the poverty and injustice of the dark age. In sum, by 'writing content' which traces the links between consumerism and individualism, N. H. Thiep's multifaceted stories remain tethered to Vietnamese culture, but float free of the political–moral priorities that make us look into the past.

Yet, as the kite in 'Lessons from the Country' 'dares to soar high and free', the brass flutes which are attached to its wings sing a haunting song:

This is the sound of the kite's flute
Does anyone know what it sings?
A fine thread alone ties the kite to the earth
A thread that can snap any time.
Yet it dares to soar high and free
For it is only a kite
That can feel the incredible lightness of life
Without harming a soul
Floating in the blue

Playing tiny flutes
That make us look up into the sky.
All suffering and even honours
You leave far beneath you now
O kite sing your song
For your own pleasure
Because destiny has already decided:
That your thread will eventually break.

This heart-stopping 'break' confirms the 'incredible light-ness of life', even before the kite comes fluttering down. In its moment of free flight, the kite is still fatally tethered to the earth. 'Destiny' *will* snap its thread, and at this point it *will* lose direction and fall.

This is why an analogy between the kite and the 'Nguyen Huy Thiep phenomenon', which rose and fell between 1987 and 1990, is irresistible. Nevertheless, this phenomenon marked a rare moment in the history of Vietnam since the revolution, when an unusually powerful and compelling picture of society turned the faces of the Vietnamese people towards a better future.

A Note on the Translation

If N. H. Thiep's writing reflects the international (con-sumer) links which stimulated new literary perceptions in Vietnam in the late 1980s, the following translations reflect the opportunity which these links also gave me to cross a cultural divide. Yet such a crossing clearly works in two ways. Translation is finally the transfer of meaning that comes back across a divide and ensures that the identity of the original texts and the translations will not be the same.

In the case of the following translations, there is first the question of selection from the three artificial categories into which N. H. Thiep's stories are usually said to fall: historical stories, mythical stories, and realistic social fiction. And the basis on which I have culled the stories has been their readiness to convey the range and quality of N. H. Thiep's writing in English translation, rather than any rigid commitment to proportional representation of the categories.

This has meant the exclusion of the three remarkable historical stories mentioned earlier, because either a reasonable knowledge of Vietnamese history or tedious notations would be necessary to make them meaningful in translation. The only major historical story presented, therefore, is 'A Drop of Blood'.

With respect to the mythical stories, 'The Breezes of Hua Tat' has been the main omission. This work consists of a collection of ten tales and leads some to calculate the overall tally of N. H. Thiep's short stories at around thirty rather than twenty. In any case, possibly because this collection was an early work, the first one published in January 1987, it seemed to me that its cryptic quality conveys an uncharacteristic lack of resolution. With the mythical realm well represented in a number of stories including 'The Water Nymph' and 'Run River Run', I therefore decided that the inclusion of 'The Breezes of Hua Tat' was unnecessary. Meanwhile, because the social fiction category is well represented by such stories as 'Cun', 'The General Retires', 'Lessons from the Country', the inclusion of others in this category did not seem absolutely necessary either.

With respect to translation itself, the many months I spent working with N. H. Thiep's texts certainly attuned me to Derrida's proposition that translation is inscribed in a double mind, that is, a text is both translatable and untranslatable. But, whatever the implications of this double mind, or double bind, for the interplay of translation and philosophy, its main practical significance was the amount of time it took me to complete this work.

Some stories made me more aware than others that time is short. This was the case with 'Songs', a pastiche N. H. Thiep wrote in 1989, which I did not attempt to translate, because I could not understand it readily enough. My decision not to include one or two other interesting stories was also based partly on a difficulty of translation: each contained more than one or two paragraphs which I might have understood in the original, but which I did not think I could in any case make sufficiently meaningful in translation. However, the kind of general problem involved in the translation of the stories presented here, may be illustrated with a reference to a specific issue: the rendering of forms of address.

Vietnamese names usually consist of three parts with the family name coming first. In Pham Ngoc Lien, the name of a character in 'A Drop of Blood', for example, Pham is the family name, Ngoc and Lien are given names. In both Vietnamese and English it is then customary to address people by a title plus a full name. So, if the 'Ong' in 'Ong Pham Ngoc Lien' is translated into English as 'Mr', we have the possibility of an exact translation: 'Mr Pham Ngoc Lien'. However, many slight, but still intractable difficulties arise, because the forms of address used with family names and given names do not necessarily correspond in Vietnamese and English usage.

This becomes clear if we consider three forms of address in relation to Pham Ngoc Lien that could be considered appropriate in English when use of the full name is not an option: 'Pham', 'Mr Pham', and 'Lien'. If we take one of the 'Pham' options, the problem is that neither would accurately reflect Vietnamese usage where it is impolite to address people by only a family name, even with a title. If we take the 'Lien' option, there is some scope for an exact translation, because the use of just plain 'Lien' is possible in both Vietnamese and English usage. In their plain form, given names may be transposed from the original text to the translation without difficulty. However, it is just as likely in Vietnamese that a given name will be preceded by a title. Titles such as Mr, Older Brother, Uncle, Dr, Teacher, Engineer are commonly used with a given name to indicate the person's position in an extremely hierarchical social structure. Consequently, if we follow the original Vietnamese usage so that 'Ong Lien' is translated as 'Mr Lien', this would be similar to calling a man 'Mr John' in English, and if we follow the English usage so that 'Ong Lien' is translated as plain 'Lien', this detaches him from the web of relationships that constitute his social context. Some degree of distortion is thus inevitable when attempting to translate forms of address into English from a complex Vietnamese text.

The particular problems of translating feminine forms of address further highlight this point, if only because there is no easy Vietnamese equivalent of 'Mrs' or 'Ms'. Married women can be called 'Ba' in Vietnamese, which is best translated as 'Madame' or 'Madam', depending on the context. But if a woman is a second or third wife she is usually referred to as 'Co' or 'Miss', unless she is old when 'Ba' or 'Madame' is possible. For example, in the final paragraphs of 'A Drop of Blood', the form of address to Chiem, Pham Ngoc Phong's third wife, suddenly changes in the original from 'Co' to 'Ba', thus indicating in this case a temporal shift in the story from the time of Chiem's youth to the time of her old age. A further complication then arises when an older woman who has never married is referred to as 'Ba' in Vietnamese; while the usual English translation for 'Ba' would be 'Madame', this title does not normally refer to unmarried women in English usage.

To minimize the potential for chaos when translating

forms of address, my strategy has therefore been to follow the usage in the original text. In my translation, 'Ong Lien' thus becomes 'Mr Lien', rather than 'Lien'. Yet no rule is absolutely watertight, and I have had to break mine in the case of 'Ba Cam' in 'A Drop of Blood'. Despite her seniority, she is addressed as 'Miss' rather than 'Madame' in translation, because she never married. Furthermore, there was the necessity to give special consideration to the form of address I used in the Introduction for Nguyen Huy Thiep himself. Because it would have been clumsy to refer constantly to him by his full name, potentially impolite to refer to him as 'Nguyen', and awkward or inappropriate to refer to him in an essay about his own work as 'Mr Thiep' or 'Thiep', he appears as N. H. Thiep.

This brief discussion of the complexities involved in translating a few basic forms of address may suggest the degree of improvisation that is necessary to deal with complex sentences, paragraphs, and texts. Indeed, especially when the languages of the author and the translator reflect very different cultures as they do in this case, there is an extent to which the idea of translation is effaced by something that is close to an elaborate act of improvisation. Even where ready equivalents in English are available for Vietnamese words and concepts (as they generally are), a direct transfer of meaning is still not possible in many cases. Interrelated demands of rhythm and syntax in the translation frequently conspire to tamper with original meanings. Complex artificial adjustments which reflect the differences between the two languages then become necessary to try to preserve the original sense in a readable translation. A method which attempted rigidly to turn each sentence word by word and phrase by phrase from Vietnamese to English would, in most situations, have awkward or even unintelligible results.

Yet, as an act of composing, improvising must still be informed and monitored by the translator's understanding of the original text. To this extent, the improvisation is not free. At some point in the interplay of the original and foreign languages, the improvisation therefore loses its made-up quality and becomes a transfer of meaning. For practical purposes, the translation comes out. The original texts become more translatable than untranslatable, leaving one to wonder why, in practice, the double bind is not far more debilitating than it is.

I suspect that anyone who has spent any time translating will have considered the possibility of the existence of something that is shared between languages, perhaps some commonality of all languages which traditional explanations derive from the Babel myth of there having been an original, unified language. But I do know that the only advice I found helpful came from a theory of translation that displaces the Babel myth. This is contained in Walter Benjamin's influential essay of 1923, 'The Task of the Translator' (Benjamin, 1969), which offers a theory pertaining to language rather than to older concerns about the meaning of words which stem from some original source.

For Benjamin, the 'essence' of language lies in the differences between all languages which are nevertheless interrelated in what they want to express. The linguistic identity of the original and the translation does not depend, therefore, on some essential quality of language. Rather, the essential lies in the 'translatability' of the text and the 'activity' of translating it. What Benjamin calls the 'pure language' is then released by the translator in the translation where it marks the sameness of languages while allowing for their differences. As he (1990, p. 80) put it: 'It is the task of the translator to release in his own language that pure language which is under the spell of another, to liberate the language imprisoned in a work in his re-creation of that work.' In this view, 'pure language' must be *the* language inhering in *a* language which cannot itself be translated, and translation must serve Benjamin's purpose of 'expressing the central reciprocal relationship between languages' (Benjamin, 1990, p. 72).

This leads to the following practical advice: for the sake of 'pure language' the translator must break the crumbling barriers of his own language. He must not perpetuate the usual error of attempting to preserve its state. He must allow 'his language to be powerfully affected by the foreign tongue' (Benjamin, 1990, p. 81), especially when translating from a language that is remote from his own. In such cases it is necessary to search all the more deeply for the convergence of image, tone, and work.

Now, in these terms, I cannot say that I have been any less in error than other translators. Something that may also have affected my approach has been the rapid disappearance of the Vietnamese literature which the Foreign Languages Publishing House in Hanoi published in English translation during the war. Since the translating was not infrequently done by non-native English speaker-writers—mostly Vietnamese with native assistance—it could be argued that it was too powerfully affected by the 'foreign tongue', although the heroic content of the works was a serious problem too. In any case, when I read Benjamin's argument about two-thirds of the way through the second draft of my translations, I sensed immediately that I had come across some useful advice. And I can suggest a reason for the possibility that this sensation was self-fulfilling.

During the time I spent moving back and forth between N. H. Thiep's original texts and my translations, I had become increasingly aware of the potentially endless nature of the task. In other words, I was already aware of the need for a pragmatic use of language which would release what was translatable in N. H. Thiep's texts: the sense of sameness and difference which was familiar to me from the time of my first reading of 'The General Retires'.

References

1. Main Editions of Nguyen Huy Thiep's Stories and Criticism

Nguyen Huy Thiep, *Tuong ve huu* [The General Retires], Ho Chi Minh City: Tre-tuan bao van nghe, hoi nha van Viet Nam, 1988.

———, *Nhung ngon gio Hua Tat* [The Breezes of Hua Tat], Hanoi: Van hoa, 1989.

———, 'Cun' in *Song Huong* [Perfume River], No. 37 (1989), pp. 9–14.

———, *Un général à la retraite* [The General Retires], translated by Kim Lefèvre, Paris: *éditions de l'aube*, 1990.

Tap chi Song Huong, *Nguyen Huy Thiep: Tac pham va du luan* [Nguyen Huy Thiep: Works and Criticism], Hue: Tre, 1989.

2. Other Works

Anonymous Special Reporter, 'L'intouchable de Hanoi', *Libération* (Paris), 10 May 1990.

Bao Van Nghe, *Tuong ve huu: truyen ngan chon loc* [The General Retires: Selected Short Stories], Danang: Bao van nghe, 1988.

Benjamin, Andrew, *Translation and the Nature of Philosophy: A New Theory of Words*, London and New York: Routledge, 1989. This is an excellent starting point for reading about theories of translation including Derrida's. It also contains a chapter on Walter Benjamin's theory, which influenced my understanding of it. As far as I know, Andrew is not related to Walter.

Benjamin, Walter, 'The Task of the Translator', *Illuminations: Essays and Reflections*, edited with an Introduction by Hannah Arendt, translated by Harry Zohn, New York: Schoken, 1969. See also 'The Story-teller'.

Duong Thu Huong, *Ben kia bo ao vong* [On the Shores of Illusion], Hanoi: Phu nu, 1987.

_____, *Chuyen tinh ke truoc luc rang dong* [Love Stories Told before Dawn], Hanoi: Nha xuat ban Hanoi, 1988.

_____, *Cac vi nhan tinh le* [Big Men in Little Provinces], Hanoi: Thanh nien, 1988.

_____, *Nhung thien duong mu* [Blind Paradises], Hanoi: Phu nu, 1988.

Hoan Ngoc Hien, 'Ve mot dac diem cua van hoc va nghe thuat o ta trong giai doan vua qua' [On a Main Point of Our Literature and Art in the Period Just Passed], *Van nghe* [Literature and Art], No. 23 (June 1979).

_____, 'Doc *Thoi xa vang* cua Le Luu' [Reading Le Luu's *The Old Days*], *Van nghe quan doi* [Army Literature and Art], No. 2 (1987).

_____, 'Hai tac gia moi trong mot nen van xuoi dang doi moi' [Two New Authors with a Renovating Prose], Unpublished Paper, Hanoi Teachers' College, December 1988.

Hoang Ngoc Phach, *To tam* [Pure Heart], Ho Chi Minh City: Van nghe, 1988.

Hoang Phe (general editor), *Tu dien tieng Viet* [Vietnamese Dictionary], Hanoi: Khoa hoc xa hoi, 1988.

Hoi van hoc nghe thuat Phu Khanh, *Canh en* [Swallow's Wing], April 1989.

Le Luu, *Thoi xa vang* [The Old Days], Hanoi: Tac pham moi, 1987.

Le Ngoc Tra, *Ly luan va van hoc* [Literary Arguments], Ho Chi Minh City: Tre, 1990.

Le Phan, 'Nguyen Huy Thiep duoi mat mot nha bao Tay Phuong' [Nguyen Huy Thiep under the Eye of a Western Journalist], *Ti vi tuan san* [TV Weekly] (Melbourne), No. 229 (16 August 1990).

Lockhart, Greg, 'Tai sao toi dich truyen ngan Nguyen Huy Thiep ra tieng Anh' [Why I Am Translating Nguyen Huy Thiep's Short Stories into English], *Tap chi van hoc* [Literary Studies] (Hanoi), No. 4 (1989).

_____, 'Modern Vietnamese Literature', *Age Monthly Review* (Melbourne), May 1990.

Nguyen, C. K., 'Left to Write', *Far Eastern Economic Review*, 17 August 1989.

_____, 'Prophets without Honour', *Far Eastern Economic Review*, 4 April 1991.

Nguyen Huy Thiep, *Con lai tinh yeu* [There's Still More Love] in *Song Huong* (Hue), April 1990. This is a play.

_____, *Qui o voi nguoi* [Evil Lives with People] in *Song Huong* (Hue),

1990. This is a play. It is also one which is helpful for an interpretation of Thiep's short story 'Khong co vua' [No King].

_____, 'Khoang trong ai lap duoc trong tu tuong nha van' [Who Can Fill the Hole in the Thinking of Writers], *Song Huong* (Hue), April 1990. This is an essay.

Nguyen Khai, *Cha va con va . . .* [Father and Child and . . .], Hanoi: Tac pham moi, 1979.

Nguyen Minh Chau, *Co Lau: tap truyen ngan* [Lau Grass: A Collection of Short Stories], Hanoi: Van hoc, 1989. This volume contains 'Phien Cho Giat' [Time of Giat Market].

Pham Thi Hoai, *Thien su* [The Crystal Messenger], in *Tac pham van Hoc* [Literary Works], No. 7 (1988), Hanoi: Tap chi hoi nha van Viet Nam, pp. 88–164.

_____, *La messagère de cristal* [The Crystal Messenger], translated by Phan Huy Duong, Paris: *des femmes*, 1991.

Wain, Barry, 'Vietnam's "Pitiful" Writer', *Asian Wall Street Journal*, 13–14 July 1990.

White, Christine, 'On the Cash Nexus and Gender Relations: Vietnam in an Era of Market Liberalization', Paper presented at a Conference on Rural Transition in Southeast Asia, Lund, Sweden, October 1989.

Zinoman, Peters, 'Nguyen Huy Thiep's "Vang Lua" and the Nature of Intellectual Dissent in Contemporary Vietnam', *Viet Nam Generation, Inc.*, Vol. 4, No. 1–2 (Spring 1992).

_____ (trans.), 'Fired Gold' by Nguyen Huy Thiep, *Viet Nam Generation, Inc.*, Vol. 4, No. 1–2 (Spring 1992).

The Water Nymph

MANY people are sure to remember the typhoon in the winter of 1956. During that storm, thunderbolts cut the tops off the giant mango trees in Noi Fields near Cai River. I can't remember who said they saw a pair of dragons coiled tightly around each other, thrashing up the mud in an entire section of the river; but, when the rain stopped, there was a newborn baby girl lying at the foot of one of those trees. This was the Water Nymph.

People in the area called the girl 'Me Ca', and, although I don't know who raised her, I heard that a man from Tia Temple did. There was also a story that Aunt Mong from the market took her home and looked after her. According to yet another story, the nuns at the convent in town took her in and gave her the religious name 'Johanna Doan Thi Phuong'.

During my youth, I kept hearing stories about Me Ca. Once, my mother returned from Xuoi Market and told the story of how she saved a Mr Hoi and his eight-year-old daughter at Doai Ha. Mr Hoi was building a house and took his daughter along when he went out to get some sand. Apparently, as he dug the sandpit, it caved in, burying the two people. Me Ca, who was swimming in the river, saw the cave-in and, using magical powers, turned herself into ten otters that dug the two out with a fast flurry of paws.

On another occasion, Mr Chung, who had been digging a well, reported that he had dug up a bronze drum. People from the District Cultural Office came down and asked him if they could take the drum away. As they crossed the river, thunder and lightning suddenly crashed in the sky. Without warning, the waves rose and the wind blew up in a gale. 'Throw the drum down here,' called Me Ca, who was swimming in the river. With their boat rolling dangerously, the people from the Cultural Office threw the drum down to Me Ca who sat on it and proceeded to beat it: 'Tung, tung.' With that, the storm subsided. Me Ca took the drum in her arms and dived to the bottom of the river.

These were the kind of stories—half myth, half reality—that multiplied about Me Ca. But since my childhood was such a sombre routine of back-breaking work, I did not have time to pay attention to all of them.

My family worked the fields, dug laterite, and also made bamboo hats. As everyone knows, there is nothing easy about working the fields. At fourteen I was the main ploughman in the co-operative. I remember one morning at 4 a.m. when Mr Hai Thin, the head of the ploughing unit, called at the gate: 'Hey, Chuong, plough the field down at the foot of Ma Nguy Hill, OK!'

I crawled out of bed, ate a quick bowl of cold rice, and left. It was still dark. Bronze rats rustled in the strip of maize along the edge of the field. I was half asleep, stumbling along behind the buffalo which I drove towards the shining disc of electric light that hovered like a halo over the town.

The bottom of Ma Nguy Hill loomed up. Leached white and rocky, this was the worst piece of ground in the area. I ploughed a furrow until late morning. Feeling the midday sun, I released the buffalo and went home. My mother said: 'Hey, Chuong, Mr Nhieu has advised me that he hasn't received all the laterite he ordered from us this month. He's eighty basket loads short; the other day your father delivered only just over 400.'

I took the shovel and went up to Say Hill. Here, the laterite can only be dug for a few metres before you reach clay, and it's only possible to dig on sunny days. When it's raining, the mud turns red and sticky, and the laterite crumbles. In an afternoon of very hard work, I can dig twenty loads. Mr Nhieu came by and praised me: 'That's very good work,' he said. 'In the old days when I was digging, I cut off my big toe.' He held out a foot in a rubber sandal for me to see where his big toe was missing. Nhieu's foot was what we call a *Giao Chi* foot; one that's completely splayed and that no shoe can ever fit.

In the evening, I sat down at home to strip bamboo which I had bought from some raftsmen on the river. First, I peeled it. Then, I chopped off the notches, cut it into sections, and put these into the boiler. Next, I steamed the sections in sulphur and put them out to dry, after which I tied them into bundles and stacked them under the roof of the house. I finally left the bamboo to absorb the sulphur for a few days, before I took out the stripping knife. I should say here that you have to be very careful stripping bamboo, because it requires the use of a special knife made by a blacksmith. It has a very thin sharp blade that will take off your hand in a flash. When you strip the bamboo, the hard outer skin is separated from the soft inner one. The outer skin is then split into regular strips, and children are hired to weave it. Each roll is twenty metres long and is sold to people with sewing machines to make hats. 'This business is not a very profitable one,' my mother said, 'but it occupies the youngsters and keeps them out of mischief.' In fact, my younger brothers and sisters knew how to weave by the time they were four years old. They keep their hands moving all day, and wherever they go they have got a bunch of splints under each arm. When the cock crows at the third watch, I go to bed. After a day crammed with work, sleep overtakes me quickly. And, at very long intervals, the image of Me Ca comes into my dreams through some small crack in my consciousness. I am not sure that I see her even once a year.

Once, when Mr Hai Thin had become the director of the co-operative, he said to me: 'Chuong, all the strong men in the village have joined the army; you're the only one we've got left. You're honest, and I counted on turning you into a bookkeeper. But you haven't got the education, so you can work on the Control Committee or as a watchman.' 'What does someone on the Control Committee do?' I asked. 'What does a watchman do?' Mr Hai Thin replied: 'The Control Committee checks on graft and reports it to Mr Phuong, the village secretary. The watchmen protect the co-operative's cane fields from the gang that comes over from Noi Fields to steal our cane. You carry a gun, and when you see one of the thieves you just fire into the air to frighten them off!' 'I won't work on the Control Committee or become an informer,' I said. 'I'll work as a watchman.'

The cane field along the side of the river was about twenty acres in area and a difficult one to keep watch over. As a result, I built a watch-tower, although, once in it, I usually lay down to read. I would doze off for I do not know how long. There were times when I dreamt I was ploughing. Once I had ploughed from the bottom of Ma Nguy Hill all the way to town, and continued ploughing up the town until its people fled in terror. There were times when I dreamt I was digging laterite. I cut off my big toe with a spade, and a moment later it grew back. I cut it off again and it grew back again. I had this nightmare dozens of times, and each time the loss of the toe caused greater pain.

There were also times I dreamt I was stripping bamboo and the knife cut all five fingers off one hand. When I ate rice I had to put my face into the bowl like a dog. That, in general, is what my dreams were like, with none of the more ordinary events of my life appearing in them. I thought that was because I had no imagination. But when I got wiser, I came to understand that, at sixteen years of age, I did not know anything.

I remember guarding the cane fields one July night when the moon was very bright. The moon beams illuminated the fields clearly, so that looking at the roots of the cane was like looking at the secondary roots that drop down from the notches in the trunk of a banyan tree. The row of sugarcane swept dark shadows along the surface of the soft, silky sand that had been dried by the wind. Every now and then, the wind gathered in gusts that rattled the cane field, giving me goose bumps. Then, I heard the sound of cane being toppled and, running towards it, I saw some of it lying flattened on the sand. I angrily fired a shot into the air. Five or six naked children rushed out. One girl, about twelve years old, who looked like the ringleader, ran out of the field dragging a clump of cane behind her. 'Stop!' I yelled. The frightened thieves dived into the river and swam back as fast as they could in the direction of Noi Fields.

I threw down my gun, stripped off, and jumped into the river after them. I was determined to catch one of the children. If I caught one, it would lead to the rest—that was the method the police usually used.

The girl with the cane became separated from the others. She thrashed at the water as though she didn't know how to swim, and tried to move upstream so that she made very slow progress. I swam after her. She turned around and, looking very mischievously at me, stuck out her tongue. I swam to head her off. She splashed water in my face. I dived, estimating the distance so that I could grab her legs. She pulled away from me. We swam on, with her maintaining a short distance between us.

For almost half an hour I kept after her, but could not catch her. I suddenly realized that my opponent was a very good swimmer, and that catching her was no joke. She had lured me along, so that the others could escape.

As she swam, the young girl teased me. I angrily thrashed the water an arm's length behind her. She burst out laughing and swam fast out into the middle of the river. 'Turn around and go back,' she called out to me, 'don't lose your gun or it will be the end of you!' I was startled by this comment, because I knew that what she had said was true. The little girl added: 'There's no way you can catch me; how are you going to catch Me Ca?'

My hair stood on end. Could this be the Water Nymph? The water slapped against my face. Momentarily, beneath the moon, I caught a fleeting glimpse of a supple, naked back frisking in the water before my face. It was both frightening and beautiful. In a flash, she disappeared, and I was suddenly alone in mid-stream.

It was as though nothing had happened. The river still ran as it had run for five hundred years. I felt ashamed of myself. There I was in the middle of the night, swimming naked in the river, splashing around, and for what reason? How much were a few sticks of sugar cane worth? When the co-operative harvests the cane, piles of it are thrown away. Or, in the wet season, it is normal for floods to destroy acres of the crop. I suddenly felt sad, ignored the stream of water, and swam back to the shore.

As it turned out, we hadn't lost much cane; just a few sticks. I sat down and bent a piece of sugar-cane in the middle so that I could eat it. It was tasteless. I threw it away and crawled back to the watch-tower where I lay awake till morning.

I tried to remember Me Ca's face, but couldn't. With my eyes closed, I pictured the faces of everyone I knew: there was Madam Hai Khoi's big round face with a nose pitted like orange peel; my sister Vinh's long face that looked as pale as a buffalo's scrotum; Miss Hy's face as red as a boiled prawn; my brother Du's face with the jaw bones of a horse. There were no human faces among them, just animal faces—not mean and deceitful, but full of shame and wrinkled with suffering. I found a piece of a broken mirror and took a look at my own face. The piece of mirror was too small, and the reflection was unclear; all I saw looking back at me was a pair of stupid, dull eyes like those of a wooden statue in the pagoda.

At the end of the year, I left the village guard and went to work in the irrigation unit. As people say: 'Land comes first, crops second.' Breaking the ground with a hoe was hard work, but I was young and strong and able to keep at it. This went on for over three years; over a thousand days. I would say that the earth I moved in that time amounted to a small mountain. But, then, my home region has no mountains: it consists of flat plains with leached fields where the earth is dry and cracked, despite all the canals that criss-cross it.

Nineteen seventy-five: that was a year to remember. My village held a very big festival. There were swimming competitions in the river, wrestling contests, and the provincial theatrical company staged a performance. The wrestlers from Doai Ha emerged victorious in the region. The people of Noi Fields were daring enough to take up their challenge, and sent out four wrestlers; but, they went down in the first round. Having defeated Noi Fields, it was Doai

Ha's day. The wrestler, Thi, goaded us by beating the drum and boasting loudly: 'Since there's no one getting into the ring, I'll take the prize for Doai Ha.' This angered the young men from my village who urged me into the ring. I must confess that I was not good at wrestling; but I was strong—if my hands got hold of something they were like pincers. Even though I did not know any of the holds, I could crush a brick with my hands.

I stripped off and put on a brown loin cloth. Everyone cheered. The referee gave a confused, long-winded interpretation of the rules. Generally speaking, if I wanted to take the prize I had to win five bouts. The young men in my village would not accept this condition and kicked up a row. In the end, it was agreed that I would have to beat two different wrestlers in preliminary bouts and then wrestle with Thi, the one who had the most points.

A wrestler named Tien entered the ring. I charged straight at him. He was fit and hooked himself around my legs. But, after more than a thousand days wading in the mud and carrying dirt, my legs were as firmly planted on the ground as a fence post. Tien screwed his body horizontally and vertically, but I remained immovable. Both my hands gripped his shoulder-blades and maintained pressure on them. After about three minutes Tien went limp. His face was pale and he slumped to the ground. The referee proclaimed me the winner of the bout.

It was Nhieu's turn. He was a small, nimble wrestler who jumped like a warbler and was very slippery. After only a few moves, I knew Nhieu planned to trick me. He was waiting for me to lose my balance, so that he could lower his shoulder and then lift it to knock me down. Once I worked this out, I stood with my legs well apart and my body inclined slightly forward. Nhieu responded by bend-ing down and lowering his head with the intention of bringing it up into my groin. I changed the position of my legs and brought my knees together, seizing his rib cage with all my strength. He wriggled like a snake. As soon as I felt him stop squirming, I put him on his back and hit him hard in the belly. There was thunderous applause. Someone stuffed a short piece of sugar-cane into my hand for me to suck. Everyone gathered around, fanning my face with their shirts like the seconds in English boxing matches do.

The drum sounded again. Thi was very big, with eyes like a boiled pig's. He tried a very skilful short feint. There were many grunts and snorts. I glared at Thi as he stood threateningly in front of me: 'If you want to live, give up now, my boy.' 'We'll see about that!' I retorted. 'Son-of-a-bitch!' cursed Thi. 'Hold on to your nose! I'm going to bloody it!' He rushed straight at me lifting his knees very dangerously. Ten minutes later, Thi had still not thrown me. He changed his tactics. He used his elbows and knees to strike me. As he was from Doai Ha, the referee ignored Thi's fouls, instead of penalizing them. I asked angrily as I parried his blows: 'Are we wrestling or boxing?' 'Son-of-a-bitch!' growled Thi, 'I'm going to thrash the life out of you!' The drum beat fast, everyone was shouting, but no one moved to stop the bout. Many cries of encouragement came for Thi: 'Thrash him! Thrash the living daylights out of him!' In a wave of fury, my vision blurred. Thunder roared in my ears, and blood tasted salty on my lips. Thi attacked me with a high kick. I avoided the kick and seized his ankles. He pulled away, but my hands were like steel pincers. He rolled around on the ground, howling: 'That's enough, that's enough.' The referee said my hold was il-legal. I said nothing. I pulled Thi out of the ring and went up to the dais where I picked up the trophy and stepped down. There were many cheers. Someone slapped me on the shoulder: 'Very good! What a ruffian!' I did not understand the meaning of that word, but I was sure it was praise.

I left the ring and went to the stalls. There I bought a packet of sweets for my young brothers and sisters and a comb for my mother, before taking a short cut home through the fields. When I reached the river it was twilight. At the bend in the river, a band of thugs rushed out at me with the wrestlers Thi, Nhieu, and Tien in the lead. 'Stop if your life's worth living!' snarled Thi. 'So this is a robbery, is it?' I responded. With this they leapt forward and attacked me. I fought back as best I could, but could not beat them off on my own. I was soon knocked unconscious.

When I came to, I found myself in a straw litter, aching all over. My mother asked: 'Are you in pain?' I nodded. My mother cried: 'Oh, Chuong, what do you go around fighting the world for? Is it shameful to make people happy?' I felt very miserable, because I knew my mother was right. 'Promise me you'll never get into trouble like that again,' begged my mother. I loved her, and so I promised—although I thought later that I should carry a knife. 'Who saved me?' I asked my mother. 'Me Ca saved you,' she smiled. I wanted to ask my mother to tell me more, but she went outside to boil some medicinal herbs for me.

I quickly recovered my strength, because of my youth, rather than the medicine which was nothing but a wad of boiled leaves from which I squeezed the liquid. When I was back on my feet, my first thought was to get a knife and find Thi. However, the co-operative sent me on a specialized trade planning course in the district capital, and, being burdened with my studies, I lost interest in my plans for revenge.

The course was for six months and my class numbered thirty people. We studied various aspects of scientific socialism, history, political economy, management accounting. This was the first time I had heard about nouns and concepts and been taught some very strange technical words. I was extremely enthusiastic, but, after a few days, I was pained to find that I was not good at my lessons. The meanings of words faded from my memory. I could not work out the principles of accounting any more than I could understand the concepts of idealism and materialism. According to me, the dialectic was an unimpeded advance, much like my dreams of ploughing Ma Nguy Hill. I thought the law worked like the mean revenge that Thi's thugs had taken out on me. Since I hated them and the law meant revenge, I had to trample them harder than they had trampled me. I studied history and completely confused the periods. My teachers were annoyed with me and told me I had no aptitude for study.

No one in the class liked me. I lost emulation points. I was the odd one out. No one else dressed like me. They all dressed smartly in the latest town fashions which I also liked very much, but did not have the money to buy. I wore brown working trousers and a blue shirt. As for eating, everyone else ate together, while I ate by myself. There was a limit to what one could eat communally, and I had to eat eight or nine bowls of rice, three times a day.

In class I sat in a corner and nodded off to sleep. This discouraged the teachers who gave up on me and awarded me five, the average mark for every examination paper. Not long before the class was about to break up, a Miss Phuong unexpectedly came to teach us accounting. She had a happy personality and had returned from studying overseas. Wearing jeans with a blouse tucked into them, she carried a bag over her shoulder and reminded me of a movie star.

'Who is Chuong?' she suddenly asked one day, as she returned some examination papers. 'That's me, Madam,' I said with great respect. The whole class broke out in gales of laughter to hear me call her Madam, because Miss Phuong was only the same age as me. Miss Phuong stopped laughing and said: 'I don't understand your paper at all. Your method of accounting is very mysterious.' The class started laughing again. 'See me after class,' Miss Phuong said. 'I'll go over the principles of accounting with you again.'

After the afternoon class, I went to find Miss Phuong. People said she had just sped off to the river on her motor scooter. I sadly put my bag over my shoulder and wandered off.

I ambled along aimlessly and took a turn down by the river, where I unexpectedly came upon Miss Phuong sitting beside her motor scooter. With the cane fields coming down to the river, the area was identical with that near my home.

I went up to her and saw she was crying. Her head was in her hands and her shoulders were heaving. I mumbled an awkward hullo. She gave a start, looked up at me, and said angrily: 'Go away! Men are miserable creatures!' I stared at her fearfully, riveted to the spot. She took off a shoe and threw it at my face. I was not able to avoid the shoe with its high heel and buckle. My face began to bleed profusely, I collapsed into a squat, and my eyes glazed over. Miss Phuong ran up to me and took my hands, as she knelt down and said: 'Are you all right? Good heavens, I must have been out of my mind!'

I went down to the river and washed my painful wound. Miss Phuong fussed over me and apologized nervously. I showed her the scars that Thi had given me on my shoulders and arms. 'It doesn't matter, Miss,' I said. 'Wounds like that are nothing.' Miss Phuong said: 'I'm so sorry. I've just had an awful quarrel and I couldn't restrain myself.'

Miss Phuong plied me with bread and bananas. 'Please forgive me. I was betrayed by someone I loved. I couldn't stand it. If you fall in love, you will understand,' she whimpered. 'I haven't been in love yet,' I said, 'but I think that anyone who betrays love is very bad.' 'You don't understand,' she smiled sorrowfully, 'the traitor is a good person too, but he does not have the courage to make a sacrifice.'

Miss Phuong sat down looking small and sad with her arms wrapped around her knees. She looked all the more beautiful for that, and I felt a wave of compassion for her as though she were my little sister.

'What I said wasn't true,' she remarked. 'It's true he wouldn't sacrifice himself for me. But I'm a bad girl, aren't I?' I shook my head. I thought anyone who could love Miss Phuong would really be happy. 'Not at all, you are very beautiful,' I said to her.

Miss Phuong laughed and took hold of my bag. She tapped it and asked, 'What have you got in here, Chuong?' 'Books, money, a travel certificate, an identity card,' I replied awkwardly. 'Chuong, if you loved someone, would you sacrifice yourself for that person?' she asked. I was confused and did not know what to say. 'Take this for example, OK,' she said. 'If I loved you, would you be prepared to throw this bag to the bottom of the river for me?' I nodded. 'Then throw it,' she said. I stood up, took the bag, and threw it into the river. It sunk like a stone. Miss Phuong was so astonished she went pale. 'Would you dare to break down that fence over there?' I went quietly over to the fence around the cane field, snapped the barbed wire, and uprooted the steel pickets. I then bent them and threw them at her feet.

'Come here, Chuong,' Miss Phuong said. She put her arms around my neck and kissed my lips. I was helpless. 'Do you know that I was sad because of a selfish man? It's really not worth it!' Miss Phuong said very sweetly. She got on her motor scooter and, as she sped off, she turned around to say: 'Chuong, make sure you forget all about those principles of accounting!'

I was astounded. I was still transported by the thrill of that unexpected kiss and, with a feeling of great elation, I waded into the river where I swam to the other side and back again. Swimming in the bright moonlight, I felt that life was absolutely beautiful.

Two days later, the class ended. Miss Phuong did not return, and I heard she had business that took her to Hanoi. I sadly collected my things, said goodbye to everyone, and returned to the village.

Back at the village, I was told I would now be a book-keeper. A month later, Mr Hai Thin said: 'All you do is eat.' I was sacked, but it did not bother me. I returned to the ordinary work that I had been doing for ten years: ploughing in the morning, digging laterite in the afternoon, and stripping bamboo in the evening. The work was heavy; but it gradually took my mind off Miss Phuong.

On one occasion, I seized an opportunity to go up to town and took a turn around the old school on the off chance that I might meet Miss Phuong. Nobody there recognized me. The school principal said: 'Which Phuong are you after? There are many Phuongs at the school: Tran Thi Phuong, Quach Thi Phuong, Le Thi Phuong. There was a Miss Phuong the same age as you, but she has already left the school. She used to live at the convent. Her religious name was Johanna Doan Thi Phuong.' I was stunned, as I remembered the fables that people used to tell me about Me Ca.

The principal could not tell me any more. It was the summer break, and the schoolyard was deserted. I wandered around the town not knowing whom to ask. Finally, I had an idea that I should go to the convent.

The Mother Superior received me. She was middle-aged and had very dark, sad eyes. 'Johanna Doan Thi Phuong lived at this convent from the time she was six years old until the time she was twelve. Her father and mother relied on me to raise her,' she said. 'Why do people say that Johanna Doan Thi Phuong is Me Ca, the Water Nymph?' I asked with surprise. 'Johanna Doan Thi Phuong's father and mother are from Hanoi. She is the only child of Mr Doan Huu Ngoc, a fish sauce merchant,' replied the Mother Superior. I was disappointed and got up sadly to go. The Mother Superior said: 'I don't know your Me Ca, but Johanna Doan Thi Phuong is a child of the Lord. Mr Doan Huu Ngoc sent his child to the house of the Lord, as though he was sending her to an orphanage. But the Lord is not angry. He is forgiving and charitable.'

That night, I sat outside the walls of the convent. With the traffic running noisily through the streets of the town, I could not sleep. Early the next morning, I went down the street to find Tia Temple.

It was down on the river, perched precariously on top of a rock-face that had been shorn up and reinforced with timber by labourers. The man who looked after the temple was named Kiem. He was a fisherman of about sixty years of age, and he lived in the temple.

I went into the temple and saw that the courtyard was covered by fish that had been spread out to dry. Mr Kiem gave me some wine and roasted some fish for me to sample. 'I've looked after this temple for more than forty years— lived by myself and raised turtles for my friends,' he explained, pointing to a chained turtle that was lying under the bed. I asked him about Me Ca. Mr Kiem said: 'I don't know. But I remember that storm; thunderbolts cut the tops of the mango trees at Noi Fields; you must go over there and have a look.'

I stayed with Mr Kiem all morning and helped him to fix a leak in the roof of the temple. At midday, I said goodbye to him and cut through the paddies to Noi Fields.

The road went past Doai Ha, where I asked about the house of Mr Hoi who I had heard Me Ca once saved with his daughter. Mr Hoi was old and confused. 'Digging sand. Cave-in. Very dangerous. Blood flowed . . . ' was all he could mumble each time I asked him a question. 'The old man doesn't remember anything,' his son told me. 'He's been deaf for three or four years.' I was again disappointed, as I said goodbye to the father and son and left.

I swam across the river and reached Noi Fields. The big tree that had been struck by a thunderbolt had been dead for many years. At the foot of the tree, children had burnt some of the roots, and hollowed out a deep, dark hole. I turned towards a tent made of nets that had been set up beside the hole. I peered into a dark corner of the tent and shuddered when I saw an old man lying on the ground in a straw litter. When he was aware of me, the old man asked: 'That's Thi, isn't it?' He sat up like a ghostly apparition, terrifying me with his wild hair and smoky eyes. I guessed that he was paralysed. His legs were shrivelled beneath layers of dirt and hair that looked like pig's bristles. I greeted the old man and was surprised to find that he was unusually bright and well spoken. What he said soon confirmed that he was the father of my enemy, the wrestler, Thi, from Doai Ha. The old man had been crippled for twenty or thirty years and lay paralysed in the tent.

We talked, and I asked him about the story of Me Ca. He held his belly and burst out laughing. The sight of his lifeless legs scared me. I had never seen anyone as frightening as him. 'Did you see that large, flat winnowing basket that's torn to shreds over there?' he said to me. 'The dragons coiled themselves around each other inside it.' He laughed again. 'I invented the story of Me Ca. At that time, I wasn't paralysed. I invented the story of Me Ca. Everyone believed it. Her grave is over there. If you want to know what she looks like, dig her up and have a look!' The old man pointed to a mound near the foot of the mango tree. I took a spade from the tent and went over to the mound. I dug as though I were excavating a tomb. When I got down a metre, I pulled out a shapeless piece of rotten wood.

I sat down for a long time beside that piece of wood. The old ghost had stopped laughing and was now sleeping in his tent.

In front of me, the river flowed. It ran on to the sea. The sea is limitless. I had never seen the sea, even though I had already lived half my life. Time also flows on. In ten years it will be the year 2000.

I stood up and went home. Tomorrow, I'm going to the sea. Out in the sea there is no water nymph.

A Drop of Blood

'Let us tell again the stories of the past.'
Tran Te Xuong

_____ *One* _____

IN the middle of the last century, at Ke Noi, in Tu Liem District, there lived a prosperous man named Pham Ngoc Lien, who decided one day to expand his estate. A new house was to be built on about three acres of flat land he acquired at the head of the village, and this was such a fine selection that a passer-by once remarked: 'This beautiful piece of land has the shape of a writing brush. It will support literature. Once literature has flourished the ponds will dry up, the troughs will be empty, and sons will be rare.' When he heard this prophecy, Mr Lien pulled the passer-by aside, and said: 'All my life I've been a peasant who has dreamt that his sons will have a literary education to help them along in the world. I don't mind having few sons, as long as they can hold their heads up high.' The passer-by laughed: 'Can you eat literature?' 'No, you can't eat it,' replied Mr Lien. 'So why be bothered with it?' 'What do you think?' said Mr Lien. 'It's better than ploughing.' The passer-by was not convinced: 'Is there virtue in a high education?' he asked. 'Yes,' replied Mr Lien. The passer-by laughed. He asked no more questions and turned on his heel. 'Crazy fool,' Mr Lien scowled angrily.

To celebrate the opening of his new estate, Mr Lien slaughtered two pigs and a buffalo and offered sacrifices to heaven and earth. Ninety trays of food were laid out all around the truly imposing establishment. The ancestral temple consisted of three compartments that were decorated ornately with carved dragons, unicorns, turtles, and phoenixes. The main house had five rooms with double doors, and its pillars were carved from the wood of the lilac tree. With an outbuilding on either side of it, the courtyard was paved with tiles from the celebrated kilns at Bat Trang. There were screens and a water-tank in the courtyard. A three-metre high wall ran around the buildings with pieces of glazed pottery and crystal inlaid in a band around the top of it. The bricks were mortared with a thick mixture of limestone sand and honey.

Mr Lien sat in the middle of the courtyard and said to his family: 'We will make the twelfth day of the first month the funeral anniversary of our ancestors. In the past, our family's importance has compared quite favourably with that of the Do, the Phan, and the Hoang. I only resent the fact that we've been peasants and commercial people and haven't had anyone pass the mandarinal examinations. In the eyes of the world, we are regarded as uncouth yokels. It makes me furious.'

With this, Mr Lien called his five sons together. 'My sons,' he said, 'I will give this estate and the entire family inheritance to whichever of you passes the doctoral examinations with a Tham Hoa or Bang Nhan degree. What concerns me is how we are going to make the world respect the virtue of this family.'

Mr Lien lived with this concern until he was eighty years old. He had three wives, five sons, six daughters. When he lay on his deathbed, his first son, a butcher named Pham Ngoc Gia, was by his side for almost a month. During this time, Mr Gia's eyes sank into his head and his beard bristled. His father always had a surfeit of bananas, oranges, meat, mince rolls, and dishes of all kinds beside the bed. 'Is there anything you would especially like, Father?' Mr Gia inquired. 'I just want some boiled spinach, eggplant, and soya bean sauce,' Mr Lien replied. Mr Gia cooked some deliciously flavoured rice in an earthenware pot, made some bitter-sweet soup flavoured with tamarind leaves, boiled some spinach, prepared a bowl of soya bean sauce, and carried the dishes to his father with his own hands. Mr Lien only slurped a spoon full of soup and pushed it aside. Mr Gia burst into tears. 'It's not food we need,' Mr Lien said, 'It's learning.' Then, he took his last breath. It was the hour of the Snake, on the twenty-fourth day of the twelfth month in the year of the Rat (1840).

Mr Gia spared no expense on the funeral which was an extremely solemn affair. After three days of formal rites, the procession to the pagoda on the thirty-fifth day and the observances of the forty-ninth and one hundredth days, he had attended thoroughly to every detail. Village opinion was unanimous that there was someone with filial piety.

After the funeral, Mr Gia ordered renovations to the ancestral temple and added another compartment. Since then, the estate has remained unchanged. It has become antiquated with the passing of time, and a few parts of it have crumbled or fallen into disrepair, but basically, it is the same today.

Two

Mr Gia's eldest son gave him an unusually gifted grandson named Pham Ngoc Chieu. Once, when he was eight years old, Mr Gia took young Chieu to Hanoi to look around the streets. When Chieu came home, he went to work with sand and clay, and built an identical model of an entire quarter with a wall around it. He made the trees with chicken feathers he had dyed green. Out of plaster, he made a very realistic set of inscribed stone funeral tablets which, like the ones that record the achievements of the country's greatest scholars at the Temple of Literature in Hanoi, were mounted on the backs of turtles. These he placed in the model. Mr Gia clapped his hands. 'What are you making there?' he inquired. Chieu smiled, and, revealing a row of rotten teeth, he said: 'That's the Temple of Literature.' This startling remark made his grandfather think: 'Perhaps it is in this child that the Gods have bestowed the gift for learning on our family?' The next day, Mr Gia went to his own butcher's stall in Ke Noi Market and got a pig's head that weighed over six kilograms. He told a daughter-in-law to boil the pig's head and to cook some glutinous rice with some special pumpkin pulp to colour it red. He piled the red rice on to a tray and topped it off with the pig's head. He then carried the tray on his own head to the house of Scholar Ngoan.

Scholar Ngoan had passed the provincial examinations in 1868. He was a poor artless fellow with red rheumy eyes. When he saw Mr Gia arrive with the tray on his head, he gave a start, ran out, and bowed twice with his hands joined in front of his chest. Mr Gia immediately placed the tray at his feet and said: 'Don't stand on ceremony. I've come to ask you to take young Chieu here as a student.' Scholar Ngoan invited the visitors into his house. He asked them to

sit down, and, bowing repeatedly, he said: 'There is no hiding it, my knowledge is very shallow. I knock a few things
into the heads of the young and trick the world into thinking I'm a teacher so that I can make a living. My house is
really a house of detention for the young. All I do is stop
them loitering, falling into the pond, catching cicadas, and
being bitten by dogs. I'm afraid you'll be frustrated if you
employ me.'

Both irritated and unable to restrain a laugh, Mr Gia said:
'Well! In that case, I won't insist. When my father died, he
counselled me to have our sons educated so that one of
them could snatch a doctoral banner and fly it from the
ancestral temple.' Scholar Ngoan shuddered: 'Dear Sir, that
kind of learning is very frightening. It takes you to the
devil. It weakens the spirit and darkens the soul; it just
makes for sadness and suffering.' He sat down looking
dumb-founded and said no more.

His wife came out in a patched robe, kowtowed twice to
Mr Gia, and said to her husband: 'The children are starving.
Take leave of your guest, and go and pull up some sweet
potato roots at Ma Phuong so I can boil them to feed the
children!'

'You've got a sweet potato crop already?' inquired
Mr Gia. 'When did you plant it?' 'At the end of the second
month,' replied Scholar Ngoan's wife. Mr Gia made a calculation: 'They have only been in the ground for fifty days.
How are you going to eat them?' 'The house has been out
of rice for eight days already,' said Scholar Ngoan's wife.
Mr Gia sighed: 'Take this rice and meat and give it to the
children. Set out a tray for your husband and me also; we'll
drink some rice wine.' From his pocket, Mr Gia then produced a small wine bottle with a pickled lizard inside it.

Scholar Ngoan's wife carried the rice and meat down to
the kitchen, and arranged two trays. Mr Gia and Scholar

Ngoan sat in the house drinking wine. Out in the court-yard, Scholar Ngoan's eight children sat around their mother, waiting for her to dish out the food.

Scholar Ngoan said: 'I've heard there's a Mr Binh Chi at Ke Lu. He was a District Chief in Son Nam Province, before he was dismissed from office and returned home to teach. This man's knowledge is profound, and he is very distinguished. If your grandson studies with Mr Binh Chi, it's certain that a doctoral banner will come into the hands of the Pham family.' Mr Gia nodded and finished eating. On the way home with his copper tray in his hand, he said to himself: 'I must go to Ke Lu.'

Not long after this, Mr Gia chose a good day to take Chieu to Mr Binh Chi's house at Ke Lu. Mr Binh Chi's house was a well-established one on the banks of the To Lich River. When the two arrived, Mr Binh Chi was sitting down to begin reading a text with about ten intelligent-looking boys, each around sixteen years of age. They sat in a circle on a mat. In front of each boy was a pile of books made of fine Nepal paper, and beside each one was an ink-stone.

Mr Binh Chi gave the students a break and sent them out into the courtyard to play. Chieu was very interested in what he saw, as he rested his back against a pillar and watched. Mr Binh Chi welcomed Mr Gia, before inquiring about the reason for his visit. Mr Gia introduced himself with great respect. Mr Binh Chi made further inquiries about what he wanted Chieu to study. Not knowing how to explain himself, Mr Gia could only say: 'I feel that liter-ature is like Reason. That is why I would like my grandson to study with you.' 'There are many kinds of literature,' said Mr Binh Chi. 'Some kinds are used to make a living; some are corrective—they are meant to mend one's ways; some are an escape from life, from action. There is also the kind that is used to raise rebellion.' 'I think I know,' said Mr Gia. 'I'm a butcher, I know. It's like different cuts of meat: rump, head, shoulder, brisket—but they are all meat.' 'That's right!' said Mr Binh Chi. 'So what kind of literature do you wish your grandson to study?' Mr Gia replied: 'I think that brisket is just right. There's fat on it, many people buy it, there is never any shortage of customers. So if you have a kind of literature like that, one that's just average, that many people demand, then let my grandson study it.' 'I understand,' said Mr Binh Chi. 'That's the kind of literature one studies to become a mandarin.' Mr Gia clapped his hands and cried out: 'Yes!' He called Chieu in and told him to kowtow three times. He also took out a package of Ha Dong silk and five strings of copper coins, and asked Mr Binh Chi to accept them as a fee for taking Chieu as a student.

After they had dined, Mr Gia gave his grandson some advice and set off home. Chieu ran after him: 'Grandfather!' he cried out, 'I don't want to study. What do I want to study for, when I'll be so far from home, from you, from my father and mother?' Mr Gia wiped Chieu's tears and hurried away. Mr Binh Chi coaxed Chieu into the house. The child understood vaguely that in taking up literature, he had entered a domain where he could rely on nothing beyond himself.

——————— *Three* ———————

On the first and sixteenth days of each month, Mr Gia went to Ke Lu with money and rice to support his grandson's studies. Chieu made very rapid progress. At the age of ten he could read the Four Books and Five Canonicals of the

Confucian corpus. At twelve he could expound on them. As for the methods of 'introducing a subject', 'developing a subject', 'introducing a comparison', and 'developing a comparison', he was equally expert at these. Mr Binh Chi said: 'The child learns like a demon. Teaching him is like pouring water on a piece of dry land; the more you give him, the more he soaks up.' Mr Gia was overjoyed to hear this: 'For many generations my family has not known half a word,' he said. 'We've only known how to break the soil, sow rice seeds, carve pork. This boy has already brought honour to the entire family.' Therefore, Chieu was pampered and did not want for anything.

Mr Binh Chi had a daughter named Dieu, who was about the same age as Chieu. The two always played together and became very attached to each other. Chieu said: 'When I grow up, I'll make you my first wife.' Dieu blushed and didn't say anything. On one occasion, Chieu was playing out in the fields, crawling around in some sandy soil with a gang of buffalo boys, when his penis became itchy and swollen. At first, it only felt uncomfortable. He couldn't sit down and study, and when Mr Binh Chi asked him what the matter was, he made no reply. Gradually, however, the swelling increased and his crotch became very painful. Dieu finally coaxed him into dropping his pants for her to have a look. Dieu took a piece of rice straw measured against the length of his penis. She folded it into three, then spread it out into the shape of a fan and cut it with a knife. After fanning the swollen member for some time, she told him to go and wash it clean in salty water. That made Chieu better. He thanked her very much.

In the year of the Rat (1888), Chieu passed the bachelor's degree, and Mr Gia held a banquet for the entire village. It was a very big feast with the traditional seven bowls and seven dishes. The seven bowls were one of bamboo sprout soup, one of vermicelli soup, one of sweet potato soup, two of pork rind soup, and two of stuffed soya bean soup. The seven dishes were one of chicken, one of roasted goose, one of pork, one of almonds, one of spring rolls, one of vegetables mixed with sesame, peanuts, and spices, and one of salad. Mr Binh Chi, who came along, was full of admiration for the magnificent estate.

The next year, Mr Gia died. Around this time, the examination compound moved to Nam Dinh, so Chieu had to go there for the examinations. Mr Gia died with his eyes wide open and, no matter how one stroked the lids, they would not close. Some people said: 'He is waiting for news of Chieu.' After that, they had to dry some thin chopsticks over the fire, prise the ends of them carefully under the eyelids, and lift them down over the bulging eyeballs. No one in the house dared to inform Chieu, because they were afraid he would fail the examinations.

Down at Nam Dinh, where Chieu boarded at the house of a singing girl in Hang Thao Street, a light rain was falling at the time of Mr Gia's death. The streets were sticky with mud. Chieu devoted himself entirely to his studies by day, and, Tham, the singing girl, taught him all about the art of pleasure by night. Chieu thus passed the examinations in third place, but came down with syphilis and gonorrhoea. His penis was hard and red, and his groin was racked with shooting pains.

Once the period of mourning for his grandfather was over, Chieu was appointed District Chief of Tien Du. This was a big district; it grew large quantities of rice, and the singing girls at Biu Lim were most accomplished. For a mandarin, this district was like heaven on earth. And when he went about his business Chieu certainly remembered his old teacher's advice: 'A mandarin's job is to make a good living. It's stupid not to do that.' Consequently, Chieu set out to extract all that he could from the district.

In the courtyard of the District Office, he placed some wooden stocks, which were weighed down with a heavy millstone. People who were put into them had their ankles crushed. The wounds would fester and fill with maggots, and ten days later the victim would die of tetanus. The people were terrified. Lawsuits and robberies were now unknown in the district, and it had such a peaceful reputation that the court's Minister at Bac Ninh frequently invited Chieu to his banquets.

Chieu had two wives. His first wife, Madame Dieu, grew anxious about the cruelty with which her husband increasingly conducted his affairs. Nor could her husband's behaviour make her indifferent to the fact that neither she nor his second wife had given birth to any sons—all the children had been daughters. Day and night, she beseeched heaven and prayed to Buddha for a son, and there was never a moment when the incense subsided in the ancestral temple at Ke Noi.

Chieu's syphilis and gonorrhoea continued to torment him. His moods were so unpredictable that his staff at the District Office lived in fear of him. One day, Am Sac, a friend from To Son with whom he had studied, came to see Chieu to express his gratitude to him for ruling in his favour in a case over some disputed fields. Am Sac brought two pots of glutinous rice, two of ordinary rice, one of green beans, and five pairs of fat ducks. Casting a quick glance across the offerings, Chieu said: 'You shouldn't have gone to all this bother.' 'It's nothing,' replied Am Sac. 'It's all from the garden.'

As they dined, Am Sac noticed that Chieu could not sit still. 'Have you got boils?' he asked. 'I've got the clap,' Chieu answered. 'I know a healer named Vong whose cures are miraculous,' said Am Sac. 'I don't believe in quacks. They are all nonsense: listen to them, lose your money, and keep the clap,' mumbled Chieu.

Am Sac went on: 'Healer Vong is very unusual. There was an old teacher named Thong who came down with wind; his body shrivelled up like a prawn's—nothing would cure him. His family carried him in a hammock to see Healer Vong. When Healer Vong asked him to sit down and stand up, he was incapable of either action. Healer Vong then bashed his hand down on the table and shouted: "This old man is debauched! He eats and drinks excessively! He plays around too much! His immoderate behaviour has brought him to this!" Old Thong's face went purple. He knew how thrifty he had been all his life; how would he know about delicious food and beautiful girls! To be slandered like that made him speechless with indignation. Healer Vong jumped up without warning and gave old Thong a kick which produced a loud "crack" from the middle of his back. His body unrolled. He was over his illness. And when he understood the trick Healer Vong had used to cure him, he was so overcome with respect that he kowtowed before him as though he was making offerings to his ancestors!'

Am Sac offered another example: 'Down in Noi Street, there was a girl with a stiff neck. She was taken to Healer Vong, who told her to undress behind a bamboo screen and to look into a small mirror he had placed there. Healer Vong caught the girl completely by surprise when he shoved the screen open and stepped in. Immediately, the girl squatted down in panic to cover herself and swung her head around. This cured her neck.' Chieu laughed: 'The cures you tell me about are only for ordinary illnesses. I've been brought down by love. How's he going to cure that?' Am Sac said: 'Don't worry my friend, Healer Vong can cure all diseases.' Chieu nodded, told his servants to prepare presents, then went with Am Sac to Healer Vong's house.

Healer Vong's house was at Diem. When he heard that the District Chief was coming, Healer Vong spread out his best floral printed mat from the veranda to the gate. Chieu ordered his escort to take the presents into the house. These were very generous. Healer Vong made some tea and offered it to his visitors. Chieu glanced at him and was very pleased to see that, despite his young age, he had a striking appearance: his hair was white, his eyes shone, his ears were like those of the Buddha. When he told Healer Vong about his illness, Chieu did not dare to conceal the smallest detail. Healer Vong took his pulse and said: 'This illness has four stages. During the first stage, the foreskin cracks, puss is discharged, the smell is awful. Urinating causes sharp pain. This stage takes two months to cure. During the second stage, the foreskin ulcerates, fevers shake the body, the back of the head becomes hot. Moreover, there is a loss of appetite and you are lethargic and irritable. This stage takes three months to cure. During the third stage, the foreskin festers, you pass blood in your urine, you suffer impromptu ejaculations, you can't walk around. This stage takes three years to cure, although success is uncertain. During the fourth stage, you are in agony, you hallucinate, ulcers move up the stomach and down the legs. In this stage you might as well seal your coffin.' Chieu shuddered and hardly dared to ask: 'What stage am I in?' 'The second stage,' said Healer Vong. Chieu breathed a sigh of relief. 'The first and second stages are common,' Healer Vong reassured him. 'A high mandarin need not worry.'

With the cure, Chieu's personality mellowed a little. That year, he opened the great Lim village fair and invited Healer Vong to attend as guest of honour. The day after the fair closed, Chieu was moved by a glorious afternoon sky to order that a banquet be laid out in the courtyard of the District Office. Chieu sat unsteadily, drinking wine with two men standing behind him, fanning him lightly. 'I am the first member of the Pham family to have an education,' he said. 'My only regret is that being a mandarin keeps me a long way from home. I haven't been able to do anything for the village of my ancestors.' At that moment, a sedan chair passed the front of the District Office without stopping. This was unheard of. Chieu flew into a rage: 'That insolent creature has passed the residence of a district mandarin without stopping. You men go and drag him back here by the throat.'

The soldiers ran out and stopped the sedan chair which, as it turned out, was occupied by a French missionary. In his drunkenness, Chieu ordered the soldiers to stake out the Frenchman and give him thirty lashes. But, unknown to Chieu, the infuriated victim, Jean Puginier, had great influence at the imperial court. Soon after this incident, Chieu fell from favour. He was dismissed from his post, and sent back home to tend his garden. His path to high honours and status was cut in the middle. He was forty-two.

Four

Chieu was frustrated at Ke Noi, where he lay around all day in the ancestral temple. People in the village spread the rumour that he was involved with a group of patriotic scholars who were resisting the French. They said that, at Tien Du, he had been the general working under De Nam and De Tham who controlled the resistance groups from up in Yen The. It was also rumoured that Chieu had been an honest mandarin who could not bring himself to support the corrupt court; he had lost his position because he now wanted to stand apart from it. As the rumours spread like wild fire, Chieu's reputation grew throughout the region. He naturally had no comment to make, and, with a poker face, behaved as though his thrashing of the French missionary had been the most righteous act in his career as a mandarin. At around this time, his reputation was also enhanced when the people at Ke Noi took up a collection to build a paved road. Conscious that he had not been able to do anything for the village, Chieu immediately donated a large sum of money to repair the communal house and rebuild the village gate. This led people to speak of him as though he were a saint. Patriotic scholars and eminent people in the region all respected him now. Meanwhile, Chieu sat sadly at home, sighing as he cast long glances over the ivory tablets on which his former titles had been engraved.

Because there was still no son, Madame Dieu urged Chieu to accompany her to the Perfumed Pagoda to pray for one. This was the grandest shrine in the country, and, although it would require a long journey by ox-cart and river ferry to get there, Madame Dieu felt it might be worth it. Chieu was persuaded, and he chose the first day of the second month for such an important journey. They rose at the cock's crow, finished their breakfast, dressed, and departed.

When they passed through Ha Dong, the rain began to fall in a fine drizzle and a cold wind blew. Madame Dieu bought fifty sacrificial rice cookies, some gold leaf, incense, and prayer formulae. She then hired a horse-drawn cart to take them to Duc Jetty. The cart owner was a miserable looking fellow of about fifty, who bargained like a prawn seller. As they passed through Van Dinh, they began to merge into a swelling throng of pilgrims. Among this throng were many old women who formed groups that sometimes numbered thirty. They usually wore panelled tunics and threw a raincoat of leaves over their shoulders. There were also some groups of dandies wearing pleated turbans and wide trousers. As these groups moved along the dikes in single file, the wind blew the fine rain across them in a horizontal spray, while those behind cursed those in front like wandering souls in a classical drama. When they reached an inn on the side of the road, Chieu told the driver to stop.

Chieu entered the inn and ordered some rice wine and dog meat. Madame Dieu tried to dissuade her husband from doing this by saying that one should not eat snacks on the way to a pagoda. Chieu laughed: 'Since ancient times, it's been said that Buddha is in the heart; who says Buddha's in the belly? The dog meat at Van Dinh is famous; we'd be silly not to try it.' Not knowing how to deal with this rebuttal, Madame Dieu unwrapped a small parcel of food she had brought along to eat on the journey.

The owner of the shop brought out a plate of boiled dog meat, a plate of steamed pudding, a plate of stew, a plate of meat grilled with bamboo shoots and spices, a bowl of broth, a bowl of blood pudding, and a flask of rice wine. Chieu turned to his banquet and ate like a pig. Madame Dieu finished her parcel of food, bought a couple of rice cakes to give to the driver, then sat out in the cart waiting for her husband.

While he was eating, Chieu noticed a man wearing a pleated turban enter the inn. He also wore a silk coat and carried an umbrella. The man looked at Chieu and quickly put his umbrella to one side. He clasped his hands in a greeting. Chieu brought his chopsticks to rest. 'Can I help you?' he asked the man. 'My Lord, don't you recognize me?' the man replied. 'I'm Han Soan. At Tien Du you once saved me from a lot of trouble.' Chieu emitted an 'ah', and invited the man to sit down. Han Soan said: 'You remember there were some robbers whom the district police arrested at Cam Son. They invented the slander that I was their leader. You searched my house, but overlooked some stolen goods you found there.' 'That's right,' said Chieu. 'After that, you donated twelve pots of rice and a pair of large bronze incense holders.' Han Soan nodded his head.

After chatting for a few moments, Han Soan asked Chieu: 'What are you going to the Perfumed Pagoda to pray for, My Lord?' 'A son,' answered Chieu. Han Soan laughed: 'I saw your wife in the horse cart. She's already middle-aged. Buddha might still be able to answer your prayers, but I wouldn't bet on it. There is a nun named Hue Lien who lives near the Perfumed Pagoda. She is the daughter of the Province Chief at Ninh Binh. She's pretty, but very virtuous. She was dissatisfied with life—didn't feel that anyone she met was worth marrying. So she cut her hair and became a nun about six months ago. In that time, she won't have mastered the religious life. What you should do, My Lord, is to seek a marriage bond, and you're sure to have a son.' Chieu was extremely interested in what Han Soan said. 'So how do I go about making a marriage bond?' he asked. Han Soan did not answer this question; he just stared into the wine flask. Chieu knew what that meant and ordered another round of dishes.

Han Soan finished eating and said to Chieu: 'I used to know Sister Hue Lien. She has a noble character and is very taken by stories about heroes. Once, when she heard the story of how the boy-king, Ham Nghi, handed down the imperial edict on the anti-French resistance movement, she intended to cut her hair and disguise herself as a man so that she could join it. Her father heard of the scheme, flew into a rage and gave her a hiding. Later, her fiance, who had followed De Tham into the movement, was killed by the French at Phuc Yen. She was so full of melancholy that she entered a religious order. Everyone knows how you beat a French missionary, My Lord, and everyone is full of admiration for your courage. My Lord, if you make your intentions known, you will certainly succeed with her.'

Again, Chieu liked what he heard. He thought for a

moment, then said: 'But this is a complicated business. Getting a girl out of an ordinary apartment is nothing, I've done it many times. But getting a girl out of a pagoda is something else; I've never done that before.'

Han Soan smiled: 'There are five steps to it. Hue Lien lives at Thien Tru, one of the pagodas on the way up the mountain to the Perfumed Pagoda. I know the head monk there. So when we reach Thien Tru, My Lord, pretend that you've got a stomach-ache on the ferry and tell your wife to go on to the next pagoda at Trong. Offer the head monk a tael of gold. If he doesn't accept it, that's it, the venture's failed. But if he accepts the gold, then that's the first step.

'That night, My Lord, matters will be arranged so that the head monk will invite you to stay in the men's quarters. You give me a tael of gold to stand guard outside. The head monk will invite you to eat a vegetarian dinner, and Sister Hue Lien will serve the wine. My Lord, press her to drink a cup of wine that has been drugged with a sleeping potion. If she won't drink it, then that's it, the venture's failed. But if she drinks the drugged wine, that's the second step.

'Now, once the food trays have been cleared, the sleeping potion has had its effect on Sister Lien, and the head monk has left, you, My Lord, carry her to the bed. That's the third step. Take off her religious robes, My Lord, then do what you want. That's the fourth step. The next morning, when she wakes up, My Lord, I'll burst in with the head monk and condemn you and Sister Lien for bringing shame on the pagoda. We'll force you to sign a statement promising to marry Sister Lien, and you, My Lord, will contribute a tael of gold to the pagoda's fund for charitable deeds so that the offence may be pardoned. That's the fifth step.'

'Very well, but you talk too fast,' Chieu laughed. 'How many taels of gold altogether?' 'Three taels,' said Han Soan.

Chieu reflected. 'For three taels I could buy six wives,' he said. 'It's up to you, My Lord. But there is only one Hue Lien,' rejoined Han Soan. 'That's true,' said Chieu. He paid for the food and wine, and led Han Soan out to the cart. Madame Dieu asked: 'Who is that?' Chieu said: 'A friend of mine.' Han Soan greeted Madame Dieu very respectfully, then sat back quietly in a corner of the cart, with his umbrella resting against his thigh. He looked straight ahead and did not say a word for the rest of the journey.

Five

When they reached Duc Jetty, it was midday. The jetty was packed with people on their way up to the pagoda. Twenty or thirty small river craft gathered in a small arm of the river, known as Yen Creek. Madame Dieu hired one that could carry six people. Because so many boats were moving up and down the river, it only cost the equivalent of a small amount of rice. A very pretty, fast-talking girl rowed the boat with a long oar from the stern. The boat glided smoothly upstream through a delightful landscape. The oar moved through the water, turning back on its sweep with a tumbling motion that pushed away the algae and reeds on either side of it. A few dragon-flies, some as thin as needles and others as thick as chillies, flew after the boat and landed inside it. When they reached Trinh Pagoda, Madame Dieu made an offering. Chieu stood behind her, murmuring a prayer: 'If Buddha gives me Sister Hue Lien, I'll prepare a truly sumptuous vegetarian offering.'

Han Soan was an expert on this region, and the stories he told about all the places they passed were very much admired by Madame Dieu. As the boats moving upstream crossed those moving downstream, everyone hailed each other with genuine courtesy. It was as though being on the river released people from the cares of the world and moved them to a poignant awareness of its shabby ways.

When they reached the disembarkation point at Stone Jetty, the ferry girl moored the boat. Han Soan led off, Madame Dieu and Chieu followed. A large crowd jostled around Thien Tru Pagoda where the air was thick with incense fumes. Pedlars were everywhere. Hastily erected, but well-kept bamboo eating stalls and overnight shelters dotted the area. Han Soan took Chieu and Madame Dieu to meet the head monk. He was a fat, ruddy man with eyebrows that seemed to be pencilled on above a pair of opaque eyes. His impenetrable appearance made it impossible to say what sort of person he was at first glance. But when Madame Dieu offered him a gift, Chieu noticed immediately how adroitly he accepted it. 'The scheme is sure to succeed,' Chieu smiled to himself. While he was exchanging a few vague pleasantries with the head monk, Chieu noticed Sister Hue Lien as she came out to say hullo. He glanced at her and reflected that Han Soan had not been wrong. He felt very pleased with himself.

With their prayers finished at Thien Tru, Chieu complained of a terrible stomach-ache. Madame Dieu was genuinely upset. It took a long time for Chieu and Han Soan to reassure her that everything would be all right, that she should leave her things with them there and go on to Trong Pagoda alone. And when she eventually did go on, it was with an uneasy feeling that all was not well.

Chieu stayed at Thien Tru to execute Han Soan's plan. Poor Sister Hue Lien! She wanted to withdraw from the world, but the world would not let her. She became Chieu's third wife and reverted to her real name, Do Thi Ninh. A year later she gave birth to a son named Pham Ngoc Phong.

Six

When Pham Ngoc Phong was sixteen, he lost both his parents on the same day. It was the eleventh day of the fourth month, the day of the village feast. Chieu had been out to make the ritual offerings at the shrine of the guardian spirit, when he returned home, felt dizzy, and lay down in the bedroom. By the afternoon he had a fever. He ate half a bowl of rice and left the rest unfinished. Madame Dieu told Miss Ninh to go and pick some aromatic herbs—duckweed, grapefruit, and bamboo leaves—so that she could boil them and prepare a steam inhalation for her husband. Chieu refused this treatment. Taking advantage of the scented water she had heated, Miss Ninh took it and used it in her own bath. Then, in the middle of the night, Chieu was aroused by the fragrance of his third wife's body. After the erotic storm, Chieu lost consciousness and died at dawn. Terrified by this development, Miss Ninh woke the house with her howling. 'You slut!' shrieked Madame Dieu. 'You failed to keep your religious vows, and now you've killed your husband!' Miss Ninh lamented her fate: she remembered how she had been duped into becoming Chieu's third wife which was no better than being a servant—she did all the housework, she had to sleep with her husband and conceal it—and now . . . now she was being blamed unjustly for killing him. So driven to despair was she that she took a short cut across the dikes and threw herself into the river.

Therefore, while Chieu's body was being placed in a coffin at the house, a crowd dragged the river to recover his third wife's body. Madame Dieu beat her head on the ground and wailed: 'Ahh, the whore! What have I done in a previous life to pay this price?' The double funeral was conducted with the husband's coffin in front and the wife's behind. The story caused such a scandal in the region that it was still being told thirty years later. The village officials, who saw an opportunity to make some money, ordered an examination of Miss Ninh's body and found that the case was one of forced suicide. Madame Dieu had to pay off the officials, and sold five acres of land to settle the matter.

After all this scandal, Madame Dieu was enfeebled by a serious illness and largely lost her mind.

Phong grew up, and, with the Chinese classics no longer being taught in the French Protectorate, he studied the modern romanized script for writing Vietnamese. He was an aimless, wayward youth. He had the whole estate and twenty or thirty acres of rice fields to himself, but he did not care about his inheritance and left its management to his eldest sister, Cam. She was a sweet girl with an honest character who, as the daughter of his father's second wife, remained unmarried for want of a dowry.

Phong went to Hanoi to study and returned to Ke Noi from time to time. One day, he brought home a tall dark woman with gold-capped teeth. She was ten years his senior and several months pregnant. Phong said to Miss Cam: 'This is Miss Lan; she's a student at the medical school and a niece of Mr Tan Dan, the newspaper owner in Hanoi. We've lived together for a year now.' Miss Cam went pale. Miss Lan went scarlet. She lowered her head, and, while her fingers nervously crumpled the front panel of her Bombay silk dress, its low cut revealed a golden necklace. Miss Cam asked with apprehension: 'What do you plan to do now?' Phong said: 'Miss Lan will stay here. I'm going to Hanoi to put some funds together to buy into Mr Tan Dan's newspaper.' 'Dear brother,' ventured Miss Cam, 'our family has worked the rice fields and slaughtered pigs for many generations. I've seen people leaving their home villages and drifting around without coming to anything. I'm a woman and it's not for me to say what you should do. I can only advise you to be careful.' Phong put his hands in his vest pockets

and, through a thin smile, he said: '*Merci.*' Miss Cam made
no response; she did not understand what her half-brother
had said. When it came to dinner, Miss Lan sat there and ate
half a bowl of rice, picking out one grain at a time. There
was some delicious carambola soup with pieces of cooked
lean meat in it which Miss Cam poured into their bowls to
encourage them to eat. Phong jumped up: 'Damn it!' he
snapped, 'my wife doesn't eat onions.' Miss Cam blushed.
With the dinner over, Phong had to go to Ke Noi Market
to buy two rice cakes and some pork pâté for his wife to
eat.

For the first week Miss Lan was in the house, she did not
come out once from her room, where she lay down reading. Miss Cam was afraid of Phong and said nothing. One
day, Miss Lan asked Miss Cam: 'How much land have we
got?' 'Over ten acres,' replied Miss Cam, 'but Phong has
sold off eight for his upkeep in Hanoi. That still leaves us
with three. We've also got a pork stall at Ke Noi Market.'
'Who takes care of the pork stall?' asked Miss Lan. 'I hire
Mr Binh, a relative of ours. I provide the funds and we
share the profit,' replied Miss Cam. 'From tomorrow, I'll
look after the pork stall,' concluded Miss Lan. The next day,
she went to the market to inspect the stall and, despite her
advanced pregnancy, checked the accounts in such meticu-
lous detail that Miss Cam and Mr Binh found it frightening.
Mr Binh would never have dared to steal a sou.

Madame Dieu's decline became more precipitous as each
day passed. She wandered around her room in a confused
state and frequently fouled the bed. Phong said: 'How can
the old woman go on living for so long?' 'Give her a dose
of rat poison and you'll feel better,' Lan suggested. 'We
don't need to,' said Phong, 'we'll just let her starve for a few
days.' So saying, he turned around and said to Miss Cam:
'From today, don't give the old cow any more to eat. She's

eighty-two. What's the point of her living any longer?' Miss Cam was mortified. 'Oh, Brother!' she gasped.' 'Think again! Don't you want to leave your children a legacy of virtuous deeds?' Phong stared at her and said: 'It's this senile old crone who has killed my mother, don't you know?' Miss Cam continued to implore him. Phong locked the door of Madame Dieu's room, and then put the key in his vest pocket.

As she was confined to her room, Madame Dieu starved until she ate her own excrement. Once a day, Phong opened the door to see if she was dead. But, over two weeks later, Madame Dieu was still alive, grinning. Phong became alarmed and said to his wife: 'Perhaps this old woman's a sorceress? Perhaps she's found the elixir of life?' When Miss Lan went to have a look, she noticed a grain of rice at the foot of the bed. 'The old cow is going to live a long time,' she said with a stale smile. 'Be careful, or she'll live long enough to bury you and me.' She then asked Phong: 'Where do you keep the key?' Phong pointed to his vest that was hanging on the wall. 'No wonder,' exclaimed Miss Lan. 'Bring it here, and I'll take away the magic powers of that old sorceress.' She took the key, put it in her handbag, and snapped it shut.

Around midnight, Lan pinched Phong awake. In the moonlight, above the ornate ebony divan in the outer room, they could see dimly the dark shadow of a figure fumbling with Phong's vest pocket. Miss Lan picked up a heavy ruler which she brought down without any hesitation on the head of the shadow. All she heard was a faint 'oi', followed by the sound of someone falling. Phong lit the lamp and held it up to see Miss Cam with blood running down her forehead. Miss Lan said: 'How terrible, I thought it was a burglar.' 'What are you doing sneaking around here?' Phong growled. Miss Cam groaned with her face bleeding into a bowl of cold rice she had placed on the divan.

Madame Dieu died three days later. Phong arranged a decent funeral for his mother, and gave her soul the name 'Doan Thuan'. As for Miss Cam, she was gradually eclipsed in her role as manager of the estate by Miss Lan, who eventually controlled all the family's affairs. Miss Lan also had a daughter named Hue, and hired a wet-nurse to look after her. The baby grew into a very pretty girl, but her mother didn't like her. The tasks of raising and educating her were handed over completely to the wet-nurse and Miss Cam.

Seven

The real name of Miss Lan's uncle, Mr Tan Dan, was Nguyen Anh Thuong. He was tolerably well known in the newspaper and literary worlds, although it was his gluttony that seemed to interest his colleagues most, in a light-hearted sort of way. Mr Tan Dan told Phong: 'Literature comes first. Sink into the mud and come up with pearls: that's what makes an artist.' Phong just nodded. The two said they made an investment in a newspaper business, but it was really a paper-trading one.

Mr Tan Dan had other schemes too. 'I've just obtained a salt trading licence,' he said to Phong one day. 'I'd like you to be in on this. If you wanted to, you could go down to the Catholic bishopric at Phat Diem where there's a priest I know named Father Tat. He looks after getting hold of the merchandise. What we do is go and sell it up in the mountains. I'll go up to Son La to find the old District Chief, Cam Vinh An, and set up a deal with him.' Phong agreed.

He went to Phat Diem and looked around the stone

cathedral. It was in an area of about two or three acres, containing a network of parks, imperial tombs, churches, and seminaries that had been elaborately constructed with an enormous amount of labour. At the front of the complex was a wide, crescent-shaped lake in which all the fish were visible, darting here and there in the crystal-clear water. There were artificial mountains, surmounted by gleaming white statues of Jesus and the Holy Mother. Phong stood and stared in wonder: 'Damn it,' he thought, 'in all our country, this is perhaps the only architectural monument that has been built to stand for eternity. What kind of awesome religion must Catholicism be?'

Phong wandered around for a while before he saw an old servant who had come out to show him in. Father Tat was young. He had a fair complexion, a high forehead, and deep-set eyes. After he had read Tan Dan's letter, he asked Phong to sit down, then waved his hand behind him. A young seminarian, wearing a loose black cassock, appeared, carrying a tea tray with both hands and invited Phong to drink. Phong saw two other seminarians, also wearing loose black cassocks, move to a place behind his back where they stood and fanned him. As he sipped the tea, Phong noticed its fragrance. 'Father,' he asked politely, 'do you think we can count on the success of our venture?' Father Tat replied in a gentle voice: 'The Bible says: "When our children ask for bread, who amongst us would give them stones?" Be at peace, my son. Stay here and rest, and everything will fall into place.' However, Phong politely declined the invitation to stay, saying that he would like to retire to a nearby guest-house. Father Tat consented.

Phong lay in the upper storey of the guest-house, while the rain pattered down on the roof. He could not go anywhere, because he had a large sum of money which he did not dare leave in the room. The owner of the guest-house sat on the veranda in a surly mood, looking out on to the road all day. Phong passed the time restlessly, standing up and sitting down, reading and re-reading an old volume of *The Catfish and the Toad* printed on coarse rice paper. He neither knew how many people lived in the house, nor saw anyone coming or going. One day, he summoned up the courage to ask the owner a question: 'Are there any pretty prostitutes around here?' The owner nodded. Phong said: 'Call me one.' The owner asked: 'Do you prefer virgins or non-virgins, Sir?' Phong slapped his thigh: 'Virgins! What more is there to say?' The owner stood up and went out to an adjacent building. A moment later he returned, leading a girl of about fifteen years of age. The owner said: 'This is my daughter.' Phong, who was drinking some water, choked on it.

The girl was just developing and too young to know about sex. Phong felt pity for the girl, but allayed this sentiment with a click of his tongue: 'Why worry? Everything passes.' As he took her up to his room, the child crossed herself and cried out the name of God.

A few days later, the old servant came to inform Phong that Father Tat had bought the salt. 'Go back to Hanoi, to take delivery of the goods,' he said. Phong took some papers and handed over a sum of money. All the while, he thought how much he admired the priest who was so young, yet so competent.

Phong returned to Hanoi and went to find Mr Tan Dan. This was the first time he had been to the old man's private residence. He pressed the bell. A French poodle shot out through the door with a houseboy running behind it calling, 'Lu Lu'. The dog went inside with its tail between its legs. 'Can I help you?' asked the houseboy. 'My name is Phong,' came the reply as the visitor produced his card. The houseboy said: 'Mr Tan Dan is not back from Son La yet, but he's left a letter for you inside. Please come in and his wife will see you.' As he entered, Phong noticed the stately furniture and tasteful decor. 'The old swindler,' he thought to himself. 'Fancy him feigning poverty. To think that he's always borrowing money from me.' Phong had been sitting for a moment, when he heard a pair of slippers slapping the floor. A woman of thirty entered the room. He stood up to say hullo and was immediately taken by her beauty and distinguished bearing. The woman said: 'How do you do, Mr Phong, I am Thieu Hoa. My husband has left a letter for you.' The two sat down and exchanged some observations about the weather and the cost of living. Phong could see that Thieu Hoa was well acquainted with the world and this pleased him. She adjusted the flap of her blouse and smiled: 'Do read the letter.' Phong took it and said: 'Excuse me, Madam.' The letter read:

Dear Mr Phong, *mon cher ami*,

I have been at Son La since 16 *Juillet*. Our business with Cam Vinh An has fallen into place. He has agreed to purchase the salt, so the only thing we are waiting for is its delivery. Could I trouble you to help get the merchandise here as soon as possible? Take a few of my household staff if you need them. With your quick wit and resourcefulness, I'm sure everything will turn out the way you want it. Some swelling of the lower joints prevents me from coming back to assist you. I hope to see you very soon at Son La. I wish peace on you and your family.

Very respectfully yours,
Tan Dan

As Phong read the letter, a sour smile twisted his face. 'Mr Phong, how do you think the venture will turn out?' asked Thieu Hoa. 'Please don't worry, Madam,' replied Phong, 'your husband is a genius.' Thieu Hoa blushed: 'Oh, you are too kind, Sir,' she said, 'I know my husband can be terribly selfish.' 'That's also the mark of a genius,' Phong laughed. 'My husband speaks highly of you,' commented Thieu Hoa. 'What does he say, Madam?' asked Phong. 'My husband says you are a *gentleman*,' Thieu Hoa replied. Phong said: 'Kind Lady, I'd like to invite you to have a little dinner with me in Sail Street. If you refuse, I'm not worthy of that praise.' Thieu Hoa was in two minds for a moment, then she nodded.

Phong returned home (he had a town house in the city), and turned the whole business over in his mind: 'The old bastard; I invest my capital, I do all the dirty work, and he sits back enjoying himself. All right! Let's see if he enjoys what I've got up my sleeve.' He went straight out to call a rickshaw and told the coolie to take him to the biggest restaurant in Sail Street. Here, he arranged the dinner with Vuong Binh, the old Chinese proprietor: 'Prepare me a special dinner for two people,' Phong said, 'and put a love potion in it.' Vuong Binh nodded.

That evening Phong went to pick up Thieu Hoa. They had a happy dinner together. At first they kept their distance, but, as the aphrodisiac relaxed them, they moved closer and closer together, until they could no longer bear the excitement that was aroused by the touch of each other's shoulder. Phong led Thieu Hoa by the hand into another room. Vuong Binh closed the door and sat on guard outside it. After that evening, the two saw each other on one or two more occasions. Thieu Hoa found Phong youthful; for her, it was like the end of a drought. They swore they would live together.

On the appointed day, Phong went to the wharf to collect the merchandise and left for Son La.

———————————— *Eight* ————————————

The train of horse-drawn carts transporting the salt took over two weeks to reach Son La. Cam Vinh An's house was on the slopes of Ban Mat, and, although it was a mandarin's house, the only difference between it and the houses of the Thai minority people in the region was that it was a bit bigger and built with better wood. Mr Tan Dan introduced Phong to Cam Vinh An. An looked blankly at Phong whose glance took in a plump pink man with half closed eyes. He was sluggish in his movements and seemed dull-witted. Phong, who had grown thin on his arduous journey, was also very displeased to see that Mr Tan Dan had been eating three meals a day, drinking wine, hunting, and sitting around gossiping. Mr Tan Dan said: 'I know this has been hard for you. You'll be fully rewarded for your contribution.' Phong did not reply, but asked Cam Vinh An if he could have an alcohol and bear gall mixture to massage his legs.

An asked: 'How much salt have you brought?' 'Eight tons,' replied Phong.' Mr Tan Dan jumped: 'What!' he exclaimed. 'An and I have agreed on twenty tons.' 'You Vietnamese, you are good at saying one thing and doing another,' added An. 'The first delivery is eight tons; I get the money for what I deliver,' replied Phong. 'Why do you say I say one thing and do another?' 'But Mr Tan Dan has taken the money for twenty tons,' said An. 'What has happened,' explained Mr Tan Dan, 'is that I took the payment in advance and used some of the profit to buy opium to sell in Hanoi.' 'I don't want to get mixed up in that,' said Phong. 'The government prohibits the sale of opium; you could easily wind up in jail. So just use your share of the profits to buy opium.' 'The problem,' groaned Mr Tan Dan, 'is that I've already bought the opium. What'll I do?'

'Oh it doesn't matter,' said Phong. 'Just write me out an IOU. We've got a District Chief here to witness it.' 'That's right,' said An. Mr Tan Dan's face was ashen.

It was hot and muggy that afternoon. Mr Tan Dan had to reimburse Cam Vinh An for the twelve tons of salt he had not received and write out an IOU for Phong. Phong insisted that Mr Tan Dan should state clearly on the IOU that the money was payable within a month and that his house could be used as security. Since he had already bought the opium, Mr Tan Dan reluctantly complied.

The next morning, Mr Tan Dan packed hurriedly for the journey back down to the plains, and suggested that Phong should go along with him. But Phong said: 'You go ahead. I need to stay on here for a few more days to recover from the journey up.' When Cam Vinh An laid out a farewell banquet for Mr Tan Dan, Phong complained that he was tired and lay down in his room.

Once Mr Tan Dan had gone, Phong got up. He took out twenty metres of black cloth and twenty metres of red cloth and said to Cam Vinh An: 'I am honoured to know a District Chief. I was tired yesterday and did not want to offer you this gift in unseemly haste. It is better that I take the opportunity which presents itself today.' An nodded. 'The quantity of salt you counted on, Mr District Chief, was twenty tons, and I did not want to disappoint you,' Phong continued. 'In three days the rest of it will arrive.' An nodded again. 'When the salt arrives,' Phong kept on, 'I'll only take the money for ten tons. I'd like to give you the other two for your own use.' An nodded once more. 'I'm working with Mr Tan Dan,' Phong added, 'but I regard him as an enemy. Dealing in opium is an offence; I must request that you inform the authorities.' An nodded once more.

The next morning, Cam Vinh An went off early on his

horse. He returned in the afternoon and told Phong: 'Mr Tan Dan got as far as Yen Chau where he was arrested.' The two men laughed. An took out a money pouch. 'Here's the reward,' he said. 'Divide it into three,' responded Phong. 'Give one third to the women in the house so they can get some new clothes.' 'There are many women in my household,' said An. 'All right, then divide it into four,' said Phong.

A day later, a train of packhorses arrived, carrying the outstanding salt. Phong went out to inspect the merchandise. He was very pleased to see that nothing was missing and generously rewarded the coolies. Cam Vinh An was satisfied and held a big farewell banquet for Phong at which the main course was a buffalo. During the banquet, An urged Phong to eat some *nam pia*, a local dish of buffalo offal. Phong put it into his mouth, but held it there until he could reach the courtyard and spit it out.

Nine

When he got back to Hanoi, Phong told Thieu Hoa about Mr Tan Dan's arrest. 'How many years do you think he'll get?' asked Thieu Hoa. 'Cam Vinh An promised he wouldn't get less than ten,' answered Phong. 'By the time he gets out, he'll be ready to die,' said Thieu Hoa.

Phong went to Ke Noi to discuss with Miss Lan his plans to marry Thieu Hoa. Miss Lan was furious, but, knowing how ruthless Phong was, realized that if she caused a scene she would only suffer. The wedding was an imposing affair. Phong sold Mr Tan Dan's estate after he was declared bankrupt and sentenced to fifteen years in jail. Provision then had to be made for a child Thieu Hoa had had with

Mr Tan Dan. This was a boy named Hanh, who had an abnormally large head and a withered leg which caused him to jump along like a grasshopper.

Not long after these changes in Phong's family affairs, Miss Lan gave birth to another daughter named Cuc. As for Hue, Phong's oldest daughter, he took her to Hanoi where she later married a man named Diem. He was an artist who specialized in illustrations for the newspaper in which Phong had a controlling share. Diem's parents ran a general store.

On the fifteenth day of the seventh month, Phong took Thieu Hoa to Ke Noi to celebrate his fiftieth birthday. Phong discussed the preparations with Miss Lan and Thieu Hoa, and they arranged for a big banquet and invited guests. That evening there was a full moon; Phong spread out a mat printed with a floral design and sat on the veranda, leisurely sipping scented tea. Miss Cam lay in a hammock singing a lullaby to little Cuc:

The man in the moon, he lives up there
Ask him if he knows what life will bring?
Life is dark and senseless too
When we heard what he said, we don't know why we laughed.

Down in the outbuilding, Miss Lan directed members of the family who had come to help with the preparations. Miss Cam sang another lullaby:

The stork flies off to meet a storm
In the dark sombre gloom who can bring it home?
It must return to the place of its birth
To visit its father and its mother
And others it knows.

Phong said: 'If I live another ten years and my business is successful, I'll have a party for the entire village.' 'Good

heavens!' exclaimed Thieu Hoa. 'If you go on enjoying
yourself the way you are now, do you think you'll live
another five?' Miss Cam continued her lullaby:

To be a man, a worthy man
Is to have travelled far
Into the provinces of the south.

Phong asked Miss Cam: 'What's the name of that child
plucking the chicken over there? Who's her family?' 'That's
young Chiem, Mr Mua's daughter,' replied Miss Cam. 'Is
that the Mr Mua who used to carry me piggyback out to
the dike to watch the kites?' said Phong. 'Yes,' answered
Miss Cam. 'How's Mr Mua these days?' Phong inquired
further. 'He's got many children and is very poor. Some
months ago he fell ill and barely escaped death.' Phong
turned to his son-in-law: 'You are an artist. Do you think
young Chiem is beautiful enough to become our local
beauty queen?' 'I don't think she's anything special,' replied
Diem. 'You don't know how to look,' said Phong. 'You
only see the clothes. That's because you lack experience.'
Diem looked again at the girl in the light of his father-in-
law's remarks. 'I have to take my hat off to you, Father,' he
admitted, nodding seriously. 'Father and son are a good
match in this matter,' said Thieu Hoa.

The next day, more than thirty guests arrived from
Hanoi. The cars were parked behind the dike. There were
several mandarins, writers, journalists, and businessmen
among the guests. A number of wives accompanied their
husbands. The gifts covered the ebony divan which had
been placed in the middle of the ancestral temple. Phong
went out to the gate to meet the guests; Thieu Hoa stood
resplendent at his side; Miss Lan tensely directed the work
in the kitchen.

Around midday, the village notables arrived to pay their

respects. There were over twenty of them, and Phong invited them all into the house. Firecrackers went off noisily.

Mr To Phuong, a businessman, stood up to congratulate Phong on behalf of the guests. The applause was resounding. Phong shook Mr To Phuong's hand and said: 'Thank you, Sir, thank you, my honourable guests. To stand in one's own house, one's birthplace, surrounded by wives and children, neighbours and friends, and to drink a cup of wine made from rice grown in one's own fields—that is satisfying, even though I know that it is all ephemeral.' Everyone nodded. They ate and drank for over three hours before they were finished. After the salty food came *les gateaux*, each one decorated with the words *Pham Ngoc Phong*, in butter. A number of the village notables used their fingers to pinch the cake into their mouths, and then smeared butter all over the mat as they wiped their greasy hands on it.

After the banquet, Phong sent Thieu Hoa to Hanoi, while he stayed at Ke Noi to take a three-month holiday. He had a look around the village and saw that while a number of rich houses had recently appeared, there were still a lot of very poor ones. The overall picture was one of poverty and neglect. Some days, Phong went up on to the dike to get some fresh air. And there, lying outstretched on a patch of green grass, he would look up into the sky and watch a flock of egrets flying into the distance.

Phong was sitting on the dike one day, when he saw a crowd of people gathering some way off. Nearing the crowd, he saw a blind musician with a two-string violin playing the accompaniment for a singing child. Phong listened to the child's song and heard some indistinct words about the classical virtues: *benevolence, righteousness, filial piety, rites*. Beside the blind musician and child, there was a young man modelling some objects out of a fistful of dough in a flat winnowing basket. The objects were children's toys, coloured blue and red, and among these were some robust figures of the country's ancient heroes. Phong saw Miss Chiem standing there watching, with her carrying pole and baskets on the ground behind her. Her eyes were shining, her lips nibbled the stem of a tender rice shoot, and tiny beads of perspiration glistened on her temples.

On Phong's return home, Miss Lan could see that he was distracted. 'Why are you so sad?' she asked him. 'You're not in love with some young girl, are you?' 'I like young Miss Chiem very much,' Phong sighed. 'Let me go and arrange for her to become your third wife,' suggested Miss Lan. 'She's patient and works hard. I'm also fond of her.' 'Would you? I'd be eternally grateful,' Phong replied. 'Don't mention it,' said Miss Lan. 'You were born under the sign of the tiger; once you set eyes on someone, you'll eat them alive before you're finished.'

A few days later, Miss Lan sent a go-between to Mr Mua's house to inform him of Phong's intentions. Mr Mua was appalled. Miss Chiem recoiled and threatened to kill herself. When he saw that everything was not well, Phong's approach became more menacing. 'You fool,' he scolded Mr Mua, 'I've done you the honour of making the correct advances, and the matter is not resolved. If this nonsense doesn't stop, your whole family will suffer.' Mr Mua pressured his daughter, while the family gathered around to cajole her. Finally, she had to submit. After a wedding that was full of pomp and ceremony, Miss Chiem went to her husband's house with the strangely detached air of one who had just lost her soul.

Within a few years she had given birth to two sons: the first was named Pham Ngoc Phuc, and the next one was named Pham Ngoc Tam.

Ten

During his long stay at Ke Noi, Phong handed over the management of his affairs in Hanoi to Thieu Hoa and Diem. One day, Thieu Hoa said to Phong: 'I've come across a poet who is selling a very interesting manuscript. I'm thinking of acquiring it and publishing it under your name.' Phong scowled at her: 'Rubbish! That's women's talk. The word "poet" is merely a euphemism for ill-fated failures. "Poetry" is nothing more than a feeble melody. When it's full of joy, there's nothing left of it.' 'Then is it all right if I tell him to make some changes and acquire the copyright under my own name?' asked Thieu Hoa. 'Women have no poetic feelings,' replied Phong. 'Poetry is made of great sentiments. What great sentiments do women have? Poetry must be exalted. How can women be exalted when they have periods once a month?' Thieu Hoa went red. The matter was dropped and not raised again.

However, one day, the newspaper in which Phong had a controlling interest, published a cartoon. It depicted a man with a cuckold's horns on his head. He was standing in a corner, and a visitor had, in passing, hung his hat on the horns. Moreover, the face of the cuckold very closely resembled Phong's. When Phong saw the paper, he made inquiries about who had drawn the cartoon. The staff said they knew nothing. Phong got angry and threatened to fire the editor. The editor confessed that somebody had in fact come along with the cartoon and promised to reward him for publishing it. Phong asked: 'So the story is around that I'm a cuckold, eh?' 'One hears that when you were away in the country, young Diem and Madame Thieu Hoa were very intimate,' answered the editor. 'Thank you, Sir,' said Phong with a sinister laugh. 'Now you can go back to your work. Next time, remember the interests of your employer.

If you can't remember those, then you'd better not work for the paper.' 'I thought a journalist's only responsibility was to freedom and equality, to the truth,' stammered the editor. 'Very amusing, aren't you?' said Phong. 'Now please get out. If I get angry, you'll eat shit.'

Phong returned home where, for no apparent reason, he smashed the mirror hanging on the wall. 'Are you sick and tired of your own face?' asked Thieu Hoa. Phong did not reply. 'You must be tired. Why don't you go and have a break in the country?' said Thieu Hoa. 'I'm going to Ke Noi tomorrow,' said Phong.

The next day it rained so heavily that the courtyard was flooded. Bubbles floated past the veranda where Phong was sitting, making paper boats to release on the water. Suddenly, he stood up and insisted that he was leaving in the rain. Try as they might, neither Thieu Hoa nor Diem were able to prevent him from acting so impulsively.

Phong put an umbrella over his lead and walked down the road. However, the umbrella was defective, for as soon as it was wet, the rain soaked through it, wetting Phong. Angrily, he threw the umbrella away, and as the rain drenched him in an increasingly heavy downpour, he tramped on bare-headed down the middle of the road. He let a pedicab pass him, with the driver calling: 'Hey, Hey.'

Phong turned around and went back to the house. He did not call at the gate, but let himself in with his own key. Thieu Hoa and Diem, who were lying blissfully on the bed, saw Phong come in, and the blood drained from their faces.

Phong made Thieu Hoa sit on a chair, and then sat down on another one beside her. Diem stood in front of them, trembling like a bird. 'How many times have you slept together?' asked Phong. 'Six times,' answered Thieu Hoa. 'Plus the time in the Paul Bert Gardens, that makes seven,' added Diem. 'It was so hurried, you can't count that,' objected Thieu Hoa. 'Seven times or seventy-seven times?' Phong hissed. 'You lout Diem, I take you in and raise you and this is how you repay me! Kneel down and lick my wife's feet, then lick mine. You are dead, if you don't.'

Diem knelt down. Thieu Hoa pulled her feet in with an involuntary jerk, but, after catching a glimpse of Phong's terrible eyes, she quickly stuck them out again. Diem took Thieu Hoa's feet in his hand and raised them to his mouth. Then he crawled towards Phong's feet. Phong kicked a muddy boot straight into Diem's face. 'Go away,' he said coldly.

Once Diem had crawled out of the house, Phong turned to Thieu Hoa and said: 'To think you've given your body to that vile creature!' He went upstairs, threw himself on the bed, and cried with his head in the pillow. That afternoon he came down with a fever. Day and night, Thieu Hoa devoted herself to his care, never leaving his side. Phong recovered in about a fortnight, but his character had changed. He now spoke rarely, and he was extremely cold to everyone around him.

Eleven

After his illness, Phong spent most of his time brooding at home. On one occasion, Madame Van, who ran a dry-goods stall at Dong Xuan Market, came to visit him. She brought him two pounds of candied lotus seeds and some tea. 'How's the market going these days?' Phong asked her. 'These are difficult times, we have to work very hard,' Madame Van replied. 'Money has no pity for anyone with a heart,' said Phong. 'Actually, I would like to borrow a sum of money from you for a short time,' said Madame Van. 'I want to purchase some benzoin; people have placed orders, but I haven't got enough money.' 'How much do you want? When will you pay it back?' asked Phong. 'I'd like the loan for a month at ten per cent,' answered Madame Van. 'My funds are also quite low at the moment. But all right,' said Phong. He then gave a loud sigh: 'I don't like women running around earning a living. Women should be safe and sound, they should have spotless reputations.' 'Good heavens, I know that,' averred Madame Van, 'but if we don't run around, what do we do to feed ourselves? It would be good if you were in the government; we women could depend on you to support our cause.' 'Politics is nothing but a foul, murky game,' muttered Phong. 'By the way,' said Madame Van, before she got up to go, 'there's a Madame Ton Nu Phuong from Hue staying at my place at the moment. She's very good at astrology and fortune-telling, and I thought you and your wife might like me to bring her along to see you.'

Next day, Madame Van arrived with an old woman who wore a long cream dress with flowers embroidered on the chest. Madame Van said: 'This is Madame Phuong from the royal family.' Phong called Thieu Hoa out to meet the two women. 'Whose fortune will I tell first?' asked Madame Phuong. 'Tell my wife's first,' replied Phong. Madame Phuong looked at Thieu Hoa and said: 'Madam, lift your hair back so I can see you forehead.' 'Now let me see your right hand.' 'Please stand up and take a few steps.' After observing Thieu Hoa's movements for a moment, Madame Phuong said: 'Madam, a taste for high living, big buttocks, a small head: they are the features of a mandarin's wife, of a life with no hardship in which everyone you come across loves and respects you. You have had two husbands. A lovely smile is a mixed blessing that can have many consequences. Even though you may have transgressed, your husband is still able to forgive you. There is a dark mark on your forehead, the vertical groove above your upper lip is crooked. This will be a month of misfortune, I fear that your life is in danger.' Thieu Hoa shuddered. 'Do you think there is any way of avoiding the misfortune?' she asked quickly. Madame Phuong said: 'The will of Heaven is mysterious. What can I say? That's destiny. We must accept it.'

Madame Phuong turned her attention to Phong, saying: 'Please show me your left hand, Sir.' Then: 'Please stand up and walk to and fro.' She came quickly to her conclusions: 'You have many tricks up your sleeve. You can be dangerous. But you have a big heart, a sense of honour, and you are not impressed by wealth. In your life, you have never suffered from privation; wealth and honours have all come your way. You are a very discerning man. You were born under the sign of the golden tiger, and no one can keep up with you. This is also an ill-fated month for you; please be on your guard.'

Phong accepted these comments without questioning them. Tea was served, and the conversation turned to the *Book of Changes*. Phong asked: 'What do you make of its principal interpretations, Madame Phuong?' 'They are not without their problems,' she replied. 'If you look at the *Book of Changes* you'll see that those who transcend their suffering become saints. However, those who do not are transformed into devils, and that is almost everyone: in some cases, not one in 10,000 becomes a saint—they all turn into devils. That's the problem with the *Book of Changes*.' Having seen that Madame Phuong was articulate, Phong asked her: 'Did you have the opportunity for any education when you were young, Madame Phuong?' 'I had a little education,' she said. 'But living in the capital, one has the good fortune to come across many talented people;

or perhaps it is not such good fortune after all.' Phong insisted she stay for dinner, and he gave her a sum of money to see her on her way.

From that day on, Thieu Hoa was agitated. Phong said: 'Fortune-telling is nonsense. There's no point in dwelling on it.' 'I'm very afraid,' said Thieu Hoa. 'I've had tidings that old Tan Dan has just been released from jail. That old man's dangerous, please be careful.' 'Who said that Tan Dan was out of jail?' asked Phong. 'Last night I had a dream in which old Tan Dan returned looking for young Hanh,' replied Thieu Hoa. 'In the middle of the night, I saw old Tan Dan hand a tin drum across the fence to Hanh.' 'Bah, there's nothing in dreams,' said Phong. But he still went down to the outbuilding, where he saw Hanh dozing as usual in a chair with his huge head hanging down on his chest and his crippled leg folded up beneath him. Phong felt reassured as he went back up to the house.

That night Phong had fallen into a deep sleep, when he was suddenly woken by a call. He opened his eyes to see flames leaping around the door of his room. Phong tried to kick the door open, but found that it was locked. He smashed the window open in a panic and jumped out of the house. Once outside, he immediately saw a black shadow, jumping like a grasshopper and sprinkling the area with a petrol can. Recognizing Hanh, Phong leapt at him and seized him by the throat. As the fierce flames scorched his body, Phong strangled the boy until his eyes popped out. He stood up and saw that the entire house was in flames. Phong threw Hanh's body into the fire, and, then, a heavy object fell and struck him on the head as he turned and ran out to the courtyard. He fell over and lost consciousness.

Twelve

The story spread quickly that old Tan Dan had come out of jail and burnt Phong's house in revenge. It was said that after the arson old Tan Dan fled to Cambodia. Thieu Hoa, who was unable to escape from the second floor, was burnt alive. Phong received extensive burns on his back, and his recovery was an agonizing one.

At Ke Noi, Miss Cam had died. Seeing that Phong's visits home were rare, Miss Lan began discreetly to see a lot of old Truong with whom she worked at the butcher's stall. When she heard of Phong's calamity, she sent some money and gifts, but did not visit him. Later, when they heard that Phong's condition was critical, old Truong went out with Miss Lan in public, proudly displaying their attachment for all the world to see. Miss Chiem's parents, who lived down in the outbuilding, did not dare to say a word.

Then one day, a relative from Ke Noi went to visit Phong in Hanoi. The relative said: 'The family line is extinct. Miss Lan occupies the family house with old Truong; he's even made arrangements to move his own furniture in.' Phong jumped out of bed. He spat out a big gob of blood, and said: 'I'm not dead yet. So how can the Pham family have lost its ancestral inheritance? And we've also got Tam and Phuc.'

A few days later, Phong forced himself to get up and had himself taken to see a well-known lawyer. This man had studied overseas and come home very expert in the law. When Phong arrived he saw that the lawyer was in the middle of a consultation with a woman of about forty. 'Hullo, Mr Phong,' the lawyer called out. 'Sit down and have a cup of tea. I'll be with you in a moment.' As Phong sat down, he overheard the business of the lawyer and the woman. Basically, the woman and her husband had a very insolent twelve-year-old son. The wife had given the son a thrashing and carelessly whipped his testicles. The son died, and the husband, who had been having an affair with another woman, took the opportunity to accuse his wife of killing the son. The wife had explained the unintentional severity of the thrashing which resulted in her son's tragic death, but the husband had rejected this explanation and wanted his wife to go to jail so that he could divorce her and divide their property. The wife was now seeking help from the lawyer.

Phong lost interest when he saw the lawyer quoting various articles, such as 216 and 217 from the statutes. He got up to go. 'You are leaving so soon?' asked the lawyer. 'A couple of dirty good-for-nothings are occupying my ancestral home in the country,' replied Phong. 'Very well, we can apply Article 318...,' said the lawyer. Phong said: 'Thank you, Sir, but there are no statutes for this business. I'll judge it myself.'

That afternoon, Phong sent for the notorious gangster, Scar Face Tuoc. When he arrived Phong asked: 'How much will this job cost?' 'We do good deeds, we don't bargain like common criminals,' he replied. 'I understand well what you are saying,' said Phong, 'but still take a small sum in advance to make me happy. It doesn't matter. Money is one thing, good deeds are another.' Scar Face left, satisfied.

One evening not long after this conversation, old Truong and Miss Lan were preparing to clear their stall in the market, when somebody, whom nobody knew, arrived and picked a quarrel with them. It was already twilight. The thug rushed at the two people and struck them viciously. Miss Lan died on the spot, and old Truong was taken back to the house where he died three days later. When the authorities came to investigate, the attackers had disappeared without a trace.

By the end of that year, Phong had grown much weaker and, one by one, he withdrew from his various enterprises, before returning to the country.

_____ *Thirteen* _____

Miss Chiem's two sons were eight years apart: Phuc was ten and Tam was two. Phong intended to send Phuc away to study, and as soon as he returned home he discussed the matter with his wife.

It was the beginning of summer. The weather had been extremely hot for over ten days, and, all at once, clouds rent by thunder and lightning were whirling in the sky. This was the first time Phuc would have the opportunity to travel far from home, and he liked the idea, impatiently asking his mother: 'How long do I have to wait for the rain to stop?' Miss Chiem did not want to send her child away to school, but she dared not contradict Phong's wishes. Young Phuc asked: 'When I go to school, will I live in Hanoi all the time?' Phong said: 'That's right, I'm sending you to a friend of mine, a professor of literature. He will look after you.' Young Phuc stood up and went to every room in the house, then out to the ancestral temple and down to the kitchen, as though he wanted to store every detail in his childhood memory. After that, he sat at the door awaiting the rain with his eyes raised to the sky.

Black clouds were building up from the east. There was not a wisp wind. A few large drops of rain pattered on the tiled roof of the house. Miss Chiem packed some clothes for Phuc in a wooden trunk. Phong sat on the ebony divan, fanning little Tam so that he could sleep. Phuc cried out: 'Hail!' After this exclamation, he ran out into the courtyard. Suddenly, there was a flash and an earth shaking thunderclap. A pile of pungent black smoke billowed above the courtyard. Miss Chiem and Phong fell over, while tiles tumbled off the roof.

Numb and dazed, Phong had sufficiently recovered his senses to be aware of Miss Chiem screaming beside Phuc's body in the middle of the courtyard. The rain was now pouring down, but the smell of burning was still strong. With a charred, hairless head, Phuc's body lay twisted, seemingly drained of its fluids. Around the body, a chunk of the courtyard, paved with bricks from Bat Trang, was smashed to pieces.

Phong was bedridden after Phuc was killed by the thunderbolt. He had a raging fever and did not eat. In a dream, he saw himself lost in hell. A large cauldron stood in leaping flames, while grotesque demons with black faces and hirsute bodies gathered firewood. In the cauldron, people fettered in chains moaned tragically. He heard somebody say: 'This is Pham Ngoc Lien here.' Then another: 'This is Pham Nhoc Gia here.' Then another: 'This is Pham Ngoc Chieu here.' Then he heard some women say: 'This is Dieu here, Lan here, Thieu Hoa here.' Phong woke shaking, thinking that the people in his dream closely resembled people he knew: Mr Lien resembled the man who sent his telegrams, Mr Gia resembled the lawyer, Mr Chieu resembled the newspaper seller, Miss Lan the rice merchant, Thieu Hoa the sugar merchant.

Miss Chiem sat with little Tam beside Phong's bed. Phong said: 'Dear Wife, young Tam is the Pham family's last drop of blood. I only hope this drop runs red, not black like the blood of his fathers.' With these words, he hiccuped and died. It was the hour of the Horse, on the thirteenth day of the third month in the year of the Dragon (1940).

_____ *Fourteen* _____

Today, anyone who goes to Ke Noi in Tu Liem District can still see the ancestral home of the Pham family. It stands, unmoved by life's changing fortunes. It has aged with the passing of time; it is broken down in a few places; but it is basically unchanged. One hears that Miss Chiem did not remarry; instead she looked after Tam. The mother and child planted vegetables, raised pigs, and made bean curd for a living. Tam grew up and educated himself. He read many books, but did not sit for any examinations or go off to make a name for himself.

Madame Chiem died when she was ninety in the year of the Tiger (1986). Her tomb is located near an ancient kapok tree in a field at Co, facing the Red River. At the foot of the tree stand three termite mounds. These lean in towards each other, in a manner that makes them vaguely resemble an earthenware kitchen tripod. People say that around them, in the wet season, the god of the waters and his generals, the turtles and river serpents, still gather for feasts that are lit up by fireflies, while the music is mixed with a chorus of frog croaks that makes it sound like someone sobbing.

Cun

_____ 1. The Cause of the Story _____

AMONG the people I know, I have particular respect for the literary scholar K. He understands our literary debates well (which I must confess I don't). There are even times when people compare his articles with 'whips' that lash 'the horse of creation' unerringly along its path.

K is handsome, intelligent, and especially sensitive to other people's pain and suffering. On many occasions that I've been out with him, I've seen him slip away from places where there are beggars and cripples. In situations where he can't escape, he becomes very agitated. I've seen him turn pale and empty his pockets for a beggar or a cripple.

With me and other young writers of my generation K is very strict. He demands high standards in what he calls the *character* of a person. Hard work, sacrifice, dedication, sincerity, and, of course, good grammar are the qualities he requires. Such strictness means our friendship is stormy. However, this does not lessen my admiration for him. It had often occurred to me that there must be a very deep reason for K's unusual strictness and sensitivity. Then, once, after I'd been inquiring around the point, he suddenly let something unexpected slip.

'My father was Cun,' he said. 'Throughout his short life

his only desire was to become a human being, but he never did.'

On the basis of that utterance, I wrote this story.

—————————— 2. *The Story* ——————————

Cun knew that death was about to claim him. His legs were already cold, and a deep chill was rising through his body. When it reached the top of his head, he knew it would be the end, his final parting with life.

Cun opened his mouth. His thirst was so great he could feel his throat shrivel. He had an enveloping bodily sense that his life was being cornered and crushed. He knew he could not escape this time. Death was upon him. It stuck out an invisible tongue and, black as night, slowly licked Cun's eyes closed.

More than ten years before, Cun was found in a drainpipe that had been sunk near a stream on the outskirts of the city. The stream was a pitch-black run-off of waste water. It was full of rubbish and supported patches of dust-covered water hyacinths. The broken cement drainpipe was laid across a small dirt road, so that the wind blew into it from both the stream on one side and the fields on the other. Cun lay in a pile of stinking rags and was purple with the cold. And if you are wondering why he did not die there and then, it was certainly because of old Ha.

Old Ha was a beggar at the market. It is not clear why he was groping around the drain on that day, but as he stood on the road he heard the sound of crying. It seemed to come from under the ground, as though it was welling up from hell. The old man shuddered. The afternoon was fading into evening as the last rays of the setting sun illuminated the creamy clouds on the horizon and swept forbidding streaks of wintry light across the face of the earth. The northern wind was howling around the low stalls in the deserted market-place. This was the right time of day for demons, and it was the kind of landscape in which ghosts could easily appear. Old Ha had lived almost all his life without fearing people, who only inspired love or hate in him. What he feared was inhuman.

The old man was limp with fear. The wailing was certainly real. He pricked up his ears and listened. It was the sound of a young child crying. Without knowing what he was doing, he ran stumbling down to the edge of the river. Still gripped by the sound of the crying, he looked towards the road, and there he saw a child lying in the drainpipe.

Old Ha came gradually to his senses when he realized it was not a ghost at all. With his soul back in his possession, he realized how fortunate he was that the demons had lost an opportunity to snatch it. He crawled back up to the drainpipe, stuck his hand inside it, and pulled out a small child. Its arms and legs were freezing cold.

The old man picked up the child in his arms and carried it back to his shelter in the market-place. He called the child Cun, which was a name people often gave to puppy dogs. This was because the child had really not developed into a human being. It was strangely deformed with an enormous hydrocephalic head and soft, seemingly boneless limbs. This meant that it couldn't stand upright, but fell over and lay flat on the ground. However, the extraordinary thing was that Cun had an unusually beautiful face.

Cun lived with the old man and did not perish because he possessed two odd powers. One of these was in his eyes, for they aroused fear in everyone around him. If people passed Cun without throwing a coin into the torn hat on the ground beside him, they did not feel at ease. The second of Cun's powers was his ability to bear extreme suffering: he could bear hunger and cold with such indifference that it seemed his body was made of some indestructible material.

Old Ha took a liking to the deformed child. With Cun he could more easily make money from begging, and he carried the child everywhere. At the Phu Giay Festival alone, he made as much as he had made in several years of begging by himself. His way of working was very simple. He would leave Cun lying on his back with his battered hat beside him in the middle of a crowd of people. That was all there was to it. Cun would squirm around, and his eyes would do the work: 'Hey, Sir! Madam! You are human beings; think of someone like me who is not-yet-a-human.' Old Ha, who would be hiding somewhere near by, would appear when the hat was full of money, gather it up, and leave. Sometimes, the old man slipped Cun a few crumbs of corn cake, the way people feed chickens they are taking to market.

Old Ha regarded Cun as a son. Naturally, he didn't pay much attention to the boy: he was busy. Just as people with other professions are always occupied, beggars have plenty to do too. In old Ha's world, the fate of a cripple didn't count for much. He never felt uneasy about leaving Cun weak with hunger or shaking with a fever when he went off drinking or gambling. The old man himself had been as hungry, as ill, and as cold as that many times. In the world of beggars, people use a child for two or three months to attract sympathy. Then, when the child dies, they throw it on to the rubbish heap, as though they are discarding a broken basket. There is no difficulty in finding another one. When you are cold and hungry, you don't care about anything, least of all ethics and human feelings.

As Cun grew up, he gradually became conscious of his fate, and this forced him into an awareness of the circumstances in which he lived. At the time of this growing awareness, there was war and many people died of starvation. The weather was very cold. Cun and old Ha lay rolled up in two gunny sacks on the veranda of a house, about a hundred metres from New Market on the outskirts of the city. Old Ha coughed repeatedly. He was very weak and had not been able to get up for a number of days. Occasionally, he coughed up blood.

'Cun, you've grown up. I'm about to die. You are about to lose me, your main support in life,' old Ha whispered weakly. 'Actually, I'm not your main support. You and I live together ... like earthworms, crickets, bees, ants.' The old man had a fit of coughing, then cried: 'Human beings don't live like us. Good heavens, why do they persecute us like this? We only want to live like everyone else, but are not able to.'

Cun listened attentively, then turned away and left old Ha to sob and wail to himself. He did not say anything. He was already familiar with the situation. He lifted his hand across the torn gunny sack to cover his belly. Cun sighed. He was exhausted. For more than ten years he had been a beggar, and there was nothing he did not know about the life of the downtrodden people. '... Who are beggars, we are beggars ... with torn clothes and no rice we become beggars. ... ' He knew how the meaningless lives of people were filled with misfortune. They lived like him, like old Ha, like earthworms, crickets, bees, ants. Cun only suffered more because he was deformed. Cun was not a full human being; he found it too difficult to do what everyone else could do. As he got older, Cun saw increasingly that there was nothing easy about standing firmly on the face of the earth. He continued to tremble, continued to take three steps, overbalance, and fall on the ground. His arms and legs would not do what he wanted them to do.

Around the time of his awareness, Cun had also become anxious for no apparent reason. He didn't understand why he thought or dreamt so much of Dieu, the mistress of the house on whose veranda he and old Ha lay. Miss Dieu, who sold goods at the market, always gave off the strong scent of cheap perfume mixed, as country girls often mix it, with a touch of naphthalene. She had a pair of small eyes and a very delicate nose with quivering nostrils. She was full of mischievous jokes and laughter. She called Cun the 'Blob-with-the-Beautiful-Face'.

'Hey, Blob-with-the-Beautiful-Face! I'll give you a cent. Come to the door tomorrow morning. You are like the star of change bringing good fortune to this house. When people go to the market and see you, they rush in to do their shopping, as though they are ransacking the place.'

Cun laughed timidly. He bent down to pick up the cent, but fell over on the ground. The coin was three bricks away from his hand. He stood up, held one knee to maintain his centre of gravity, and reached out with his free hand. Again, however, he fell obliquely to the right. The coin was now a further brick away from Cun. Miss Dieu laughed like a butterfly on the veranda of the house: 'Hey, Blob-with-the-Beautiful-Face! You missed by a long way. Try and get up! Try once more and see how you fare!'

Cun was so pleased he laughed. Good heavens, he'd made her happy. Cun stood up. He tried to hold both knees. That seemed to work. That's it, that's it.... All he had to do was to try a little harder and lean over to the left so that he could reach the coin. He gasped and broke out into a sweat. Cun estimated the distance and smiled. Then, at the same moment as he leant out to pick up the coin, Dieu jumped down and moved the coin one brick to the side. She shrieked with laughter. Cun lost his poise and fell down. He smashed his head on the bricks and, although he was bleeding from the mouth, he ignored his injury. The woman's attractive nose made him suck in his breath as quickly as he could. She had never been as close to Cun as that.

Cun laughed heartily. If he had known how, he would have sung.

Old Ha sat quietly at the corner of the broken wall feeling pity as he looked at Cun. The old man stood up sluggishly, went over to the coin, picked it up, and put it into his pocket. Dieu stopped laughing. 'You miserable old man,' she snapped as her lips tightened impertinently. 'The coin wasn't for you at all! I'm sure you'll spend it on drink.'

Old Ha stood crestfallen like someone who had done something wrong and expected a thrashing. Dieu disappeared into the house, while old Ha squatted down and wiped the blood off Cun's mouth. He picked Cun up by the armpit and guided him towards the market.

Miss Dieu had gradually worked her way into Cun's life. He thought about her endlessly. He visualized her every move, heard her voice, imagined her laughter. He paid no attention to old Ha's tear-choked utterances as he lay beside him. Some time later, old Ha vomited and, as he did so, he pinched Cun's face so hard with his gnarled fingers that the burning pain suddenly brought Cun back to his senses. Cun opened his eyes. He was startled to see that old Ha's face had completely changed. It was waxen and distorted, so that the vertical flute above the upper-lip was tilted to one side. From out of the old man's mouth there lapped a flow of black blood. He tried incoherently to say something. He tried to press a small purse into Cun's hand. Cun crawled to his feet. He understood what had happened: death was appearing before him. It was there. It lurked very deep in the pupils of the old man's eyes and killed the colour in them. Cun sobbed. Although he was only very dimly aware of it, he had lost his mainstay, the mainstay of his earthly existence.

After old Ha's death, Cun's fate did not change radically. He was still hungry and cold. But, in the terrible winter of that year, Dieu married an unfeeling young man who carried merchandise. Cun followed every detail of her life, and his observations made him feel that she was not very happy.

Cun was not deceived. Three months after the wedding, the husband made off with his new wife's property and fled to the south with a lover. Dieu had lost everything. She fell ill and was so unhappy there were times when she contemplated suicide.

Nevertheless, her spirits eventually started to lift. The day that her illness seemed to pass and she began to recover her appetite was a gentle summer day. She sat in her room, looking out into the street. The sunlight shimmered on the canopies of the shady fig trees, the mango trees, and the ornamental shrubs. Nobody else was at home, and all that could be heard was the disconcerting sound of wood-borers grinding away in the corner of an empty closet.

Miss Dieu thought of the market and her small-goods shop. She wondered when she would be able to have another shop like that. She looked sadly out into the street. Then, suddenly, she saw Cun sitting up on the veranda, outside the door of her house. He was feeling for something with his hand in a purse. Miss Dieu kneeled down and looked out of the window as Cun opened a cloth envelope that old Ha had given him. The envelope was made of dark brown cloth with black stitching and was as small as a chicken's gizzard. Miss Dieu gave a sudden start when she saw some gold rings glittering in the palm of Cun's hand. She felt a chill run down her spine. Her arms and legs shuddered violently, and a thought flashed through her mind.

'Hey, Blob-with-the-Beautiful-Face!' She hurriedly pushed the door ajar and squatted down beside Cun. 'What have you got in your hand there?'

Cun raised his head, stretched out his hand, and said in a tone of spontaneous pride: 'Rings. These are the gold rings old Ha gave me.'

'Real gold or fool's gold?' Miss Dieu inquired as she grabbed Cun's hand. 'Let me have a look,' she said, now holding three rather heavy rings in her hand. 'Let me have a look.'

Miss Dieu took each ring and let it fall gently on to a slab of stone. She listened carefully. She held the rings up so that they flashed in the sunlight. She put them into her mouth and bit them. 'Good heavens, it's real gold,' she gasped. 'There's a whole family inheritance here. This Blob-with-the-Beautiful-Face is truly rich.' She blanched, laughed, cried, and thumped Cun's body repeatedly with her small fist. ' "Real gold is not brass. Don't test it in the flame that burns a golden heart." You little puppy! How is it that I haven't known you till now?'

Cun, whose face had broken into a euphoric smile, swooned with bliss. 'Come in here, come in here, you rich little puppy,' Miss Dieu panted, as she closed the door and pressed Cun's body down into a chair. She put on the rings, then clasped her hands behind her. She stood right up close in front of Cun's face, and arched her body like a bow in front of him.

'Now? I'll bargain, OK!' Miss Dieu laughed. She spoke with her thoughts sparking like lightning flashes in her brain. 'You must first give me these three rings. It doesn't matter if you don't have them. You are still a beggar. How about it? Do you agree? I'll give you whatever you want.'

Cun nodded with the corners of his eyes full of tears. He felt only pleasure, for he had made her happy. She had recovered. She was strong. Cun was enraptured.

'How about it?' she cajoled, as she bent down and rubbed her forehead against Cun's. 'What are you looking like that for?' She pealed with laughter. 'Tell me, tell me. What do you want now?' Cun raised his hand, but only made a vague gesture in space, because he was unable to activate the sinews in his arm. People who light incense sticks in front of an altar also make gestures like that.

'All right, I understand now,' Miss Dieu said. She sat down beside Cun and fondled him. 'You are also a bastard! You men are all the same.... But it's OK.... It's all right. That's the price we women must pay. It's OK. I'm only afraid that you can't perform, that an ill-bred husband of mine still can't make me pregnant.'

Miss Dieu pulled Cun out of the chair and slammed him on to the bed. Cun was terrified. He screwed his eyes closed and pushed his face down on to Dieu's quivering, vaguely blue, translucent nose. He was like someone flying in the clouds. He suddenly felt all the bitterness of his life flow away in a flood of unknown relief.

In the end, Cun had forgotten about all the time he had spent sitting in the street. 'That means we're square!' He could hear the sound of Miss Dieu's voice somewhere; he understood that he had just experienced something really wonderful; he felt empty, but had a sense of surpassing exaltation that dizzied and dazzled him.

Cun did not comprehend that this was the only opportunity he would have in his miserable life to experience this feeling. But this opportunity, in all its strangeness, would give Cun a son in nine months' time.

Nine months later, Miss Dieu gave birth to a son. Some months before, she had said to Cun: 'Hey, Blob-with-the-Beautiful-Face, you are about to have a child! I couldn't have believed that anything as strange as this would have happened either.'

Cun was so happy he was beside himself. He didn't eat or drink, and all that was left of him was skin and bones. He could not believe he was going to have a child. Someone who was not-yet-a-human-being could still have a child. Cun visualized it very clearly: it would move strongly across the face of the earth, it would never lose its balance, it would smile as it went through life, it would wear a halo shining with many colours.

Cun lived in an agitated state during the last months of Miss Dieu's pregnancy. He became seriously ill; his greatest fear was that death would strike him before he knew what the child was like. He prayed daily for death's forbearance, and his prayers were answered. Death would wait until the minute his son was born, so that he could take his place on earth.

On exactly the day that Miss Dieu gave birth, Cun crawled from his stall in the market to the window of her house. It was drizzling, and the penetrating cold numbed Cun's body. His head was burning—from time to time, he passed out. Only a little over 100 metres was a great distance for Cun. Every metre he dragged himself along the road he struggled with death. It was there, as black as the night falling around him. Cun continued to edge himself along, metre by metre, as it pulled him back down into the mud.

While he dragged himself along with blood oozing out of his ear, he groaned. He reached the veranda outside the lamplight in the window and fainted. When he regained consciousness, Cun felt as though some immense object was pressing on his body.

Cun opened his mouth. Thirst. His throat felt dry. In all his weary life as a beggar, he had never been as thirsty as this. He tried to hold his breath to regain his strength. Alternatively, he passed out and regained consciousness, while he waited for a sign that his child was born. Then, in the middle of the night, Cun was suddenly startled by the sound of a trembling cry inside the house. It was the wailing of a newborn baby boy. Cun knew that his child was born.

Cun smiled blissfully and sank into unconsciousness. A very light wisp of wind glided over Cun's still face.

Cun was dead. It had really been short, this life of some-one who was not-yet-a-human-being. It was the winter of the great famine of 1944.

3. Conclusion

After I'd finished writing Cun's story, I took it and read it to the literary critic K. He turned pale as the story unfolded.

'That's not correct!' he said, pulling the manuscript out of my hand. 'You've fabricated the story! You need to get it straight. The reality was very different. How could you know what my father was like?'

K searched somewhere in the bookcase and found a pile of photographs. He flicked through the portraits for a moment, then pulled out a colour photo. He gave a gentle laugh that built up and faded away, while his soft hand touched the pressure point behind my elbow: 'My father was Cun, but he wasn't like that! Do you see? This is my father's photo here!'

The photo was of a big fat man wearing a black silk shirt with a starched collar. He also wore a neatly trimmed moustache and was smiling at me.

The General Retires

_____ *One* _____

WHEN I wrote these lines I stirred up some emotions which
time had effaced in a few friends of mine, and went as far as
to disturb the peace of my father's grave. I was forced to do
this by a feeling that I had to defend my father's memory,
and it is for this reason that I ask my readers to forgive my
inadequate pen.

My father, Thuan, was the oldest child of the Nguyen
family. The Nguyen family was a very large one, and its
male descendants outnumbered those of all the other famil-
ies in the village, except possibly for the Vu. My grandfather had left the village to become a Confucian scholar
and later returned to teach. He had two wives. His first wife
died a few days after giving birth to my father, and so he
remarried. His second wife was a cloth dyer. I never set eyes
on her. All that I heard about her was that she was a very
cruel woman. Living with his step-mother, my father had
such a bitter childhood that he ran away from home when
he was twelve. He joined the army and rarely came home.

Of course, after several years, he came back to the village
to get married. But this marriage was certainly not a love
match. He had ten days' leave and a great deal of business to
attend to. Love has certain requirements, and among these is
time.

As I grew up, I didn't know anything about my father at

all. I'm sure my mother knew just as little about him, for his whole life had been devoted to war.

I got a job, married, had children. My mother aged. My father was still away on far-flung campaigns. Now and then, he passed by, but his visits were always short. His letters were also short, although reading between the lines I felt they contained a lot of love and concern.

I was the first child, and I have to thank my father for everything. I was able to study and to travel overseas. The material well-being of the family was also due to the arrangements he made. My house is on the outskirts of Hanoi. It was built eight years before my father retired. It's a handsome, but rather uncomfortable country house. I built it from the plans of a well-known architect who was a friend of my father. He was a colonel whose only experience was in building barracks.

At the age of seventy, my father retired with the rank of Major-General.

Even though I knew he was about to retire, I was still amazed when he came home. My mother was already senile (she was six years older than my father), and so I was the only one with special feelings about his return. The children were still young, and my wife knew very little about him because we married when he was out of contact with us for a long time during the war. Nevertheless, my father always had a position of honour and pride in the family. All the relatives and everyone else in the village placed great store on his reputation.

My father returned home with very few belongings. He was in good health. He said: 'My life's work is over.' I said: 'Yes.' He laughed. A mood of excitement spread throughout the house, and the long drawn-out welcome home left everyone overwrought for a couple of weeks. With our life in disorder, there were days when we didn't eat the evening meal until midnight. Visitors flocked to the house. My wife said: 'This can't go on.' I had a pig slaughtered and went to invite everyone in the village to share in the excitement. Although my village is near the city, the customs of the countryside are still very strong.

It wasn't until a month later that I finally had the opportunity to sit down and have a family discussion with my father.

Two

Before I continue with the story, permit me to say something about my family.

I am thirty-seven years old, and I work as an engineer at the Physics Institute. My wife, Thuy, is a doctor at the Maternity Hospital. We have two daughters, one fourteen, one twelve. As I've indicated, my old mother is muddled and spends her time sitting in the same place all day.

Apart from this, the household includes Mr Co and Miss Lai, his dotty daughter.

Mr Co is sixty years old and comes from Thanh Hoa. My wife met him and his daughter after a fire had burnt down their house and left them destitute. Because my wife felt they were good people, she took pity on them and arranged for them to live with us. They live separately down in the outbuilding and keep to themselves, but my wife provides for them. They are not registered inhabitants of the household, and so, like other people in the city, they aren't eligible for the provision of basic rations and necessities from the state.

Mr Co is gentle and patient. He takes responsibility for the garden, the pigs, the chickens, and the dogs. My wife has a business raising Alsatian dogs. At the beginning, I didn't suspect that this business would be so profitable. However, it has become our main source of income. Although Miss Lai is simple, she is still able to work hard and is good at household chores. My wife taught her how to cook pork crackling and mushrooms and braised chicken. Miss Lai said: 'I never eat that kind of food.' It's true, she doesn't either.

Neither my wife and I nor the children have to worry about housework. Everything from the cooking to the washing is given to Mr Co and his daughter to attend to. My wife keeps a tight rein on our expenses. I'm always busy with something and I'm presently devoting myself to an engineering project that involves the application of electrolysis.

There is something else I should say: the relationship between my wife and me is amicable. Thuy is well educated and lives the life of a modern woman. We each have our own way of thinking, and our views on life are relatively simple. Thuy is as well in control of the family economy as she is of the children's education. As for me, it seems to me that I'm old-fashioned, awkward, and full of contradictions.

Three

To return to the family discussion I was having with my father. He said: 'Now that I'm retired, what shall I do?' 'Write your memoirs,' I suggested. 'No!' he replied. 'Breed parrots,' said my wife. Around town, many people were breeding parrots and nightingales. 'Breed them to make money?' my father asked. My wife didn't answer. 'We'll see!' said my father.

He gave everyone in the house, including Mr Co and

Miss Lai, four metres of military cloth. 'You are very egal-itarian,' I joked. 'That's my rule of life,' he replied. My wife said: 'With everyone in a uniform the house will become a barracks.' Everyone burst out laughing.

My father wanted to live in a room in the outbuilding like my mother, but my wife wouldn't hear of it. This sad-dened my father. It troubled him that my mother lived and ate by herself. 'This is because she is disturbed,' my wife explained. My father brooded.

I couldn't understand why my two daughters rarely went near their grandfather. I let them study foreign languages and music. They were always busy. On one occasion my father said: 'What books have you girls got for me to read?' Mi smiled and Vi said: 'What do you like to read, Grandfather?' 'Whatever's easy,' replied my father. 'We haven't got any books like that,' the girls said in unison. I took out a subscription for the daily paper for him. He didn't like literature—he found today's literary styles difficult to appreciate.

One day when I got home from work, my father was standing near the row of kennels and chicken coups my wife had set up for her business. I could see he was not happy and said: 'What's the matter?' 'Mr Co and Miss Lai have a very hard life,' he answered. 'Their work is never finished. I want to give them a hand, if it's all right.' 'Let me ask Thuy,' I said. 'Father was a general,' replied my wife. 'Now that he has retired he is still a general. Father is a commander; if he acts like an ordinary soldier, everything will be thrown into disorder.' My father said nothing.

Although my father was retired, he had many visitors. This surprised and pleased me. But my wife said: 'Don't be so glad, Father. They are only relying on you for help. Don't tire yourself.' My father laughed: 'It's nothing at all. I'm only writing letters like this one: "Dear N, Commander in Chief of Military District. . . . I'm writing this letter to you, etc. . . . in over fifty years this is the first time I have celebrated the third day of the third month under my own roof. When we were out on the battlefield, we often dreamed, etc. . . . Do you remember the village on the side of the road where Miss Hue made some dumplings with mouldy flour? She got it all over her, even her back. . . . There is a person here I know named M. who wants to work under your command, etc. . . ." Can't I write letters like that?' I said: 'Yes.' My wife said: 'No, you can't!' My father scratched his chin. 'It's only a small request they're asking of me,' he said.

My father usually put his letters in stiff official envelopes, 20 cm by 30 cm, marked 'Ministry of National Defence', and gave them to someone reliable to deliver. After three months, he was out of official envelopes. He then made his own with exercise book covers of the same size, 20 cm by 30 cm. A year later, he put his letters into the ordinary envelopes that are on sale at the post office counter at ten for five dong.

In July of that year, that is three months after my father retired, one of my uncles, Mr Bong, held a wedding for his son.

Four

Mr Bong and my father are half-brothers. Bong's son, Tuan, works an ox-cart. Both Bong and his son are alarming characters: they're as big as giants and they talk like daredevils. This was Tuan's second marriage. His first wife wouldn't take his beatings any more and left him. In court he testified that she had left him for someone else, and the court was forced to release him. His wife-to-be, Kim Chi, taught at a kindergarten. She was from a well-educated family, but had somehow got involved with him. It was said he'd made her pregnant. Kim Chi is a beautiful girl, and as Tuan's wife it was certainly a case of 'a sprig of jasmine in a field of buffalo shit'. Basically, we aren't fond of Mr Bong and his son. The trouble is that blood is thicker than water, and we can't avoid them on important anniversaries and festivals. Nevertheless, we ignore them most of the time.

Bong likes to say: 'Damn these intellectuals! They despise working people! It's only because I have respect for their father that I haven't kept clear of their house.' Even though he spoke like this, Bong still came to borrow money. My wife was strict and always forced him to sign a security note. This made him very indignant. He'd say: 'I'm their uncle, yet if I overlook a debt they behave just like landlords.' He still overlooked many of his debts.

Bong talked with my father about his son's wedding: 'You must act as the Master of Ceremonies. Kim Chi's father is a Deputy Chief of a Department, you are a General, you two are of "the same social class". The bride and groom need to have your blessing. What value am I as an ox-cart coolie?' My father consented. The wedding on the edge of the city was a ridiculous vulgar affair. Three cars. Filtered cigarettes that were replaced by roll-your-owns towards the end of the dinner. There were fifty trays of food but twelve were left untouched. The bridegroom wore a black suit and a red tie. I had to lend him the best tie in my wardrobe. I say 'lend', but I wasn't sure I'd ever get it back. The best men were six youths wearing identical khaki outfits and wild beards. At the beginning of the wedding the orchestra played 'Ave Maria'. One fellow from the same ox-cart co-operative as Tuan jumped up and sang a frightful solo:

O ... eh ... my poor little roasted chicken
I've wandered all over the world
Looking to find some money
O money, fall into my pocket
O ... eh ... my sad little roasted chicken.

After that it was my father's turn. He was bewildered and miserable. He had overprepared his speech. A clarinet punctuated each sentence by blaring stupidly after each full stop. Firecrackers went off noisily. Young children provided a nonsensical commentary. My father held the paper so tightly his body trembled, and he skipped over a number of paragraphs. He was hurt and frightened by the motley mob that milled around and was rudely indifferent to his speech. His new relative, the Deputy Department Chief, also became frightened, and spilt wine all over the bride's dress. You couldn't hear a thing. The raw band drowned everything out with happy songs from the Beatles and Abba.

After that, my father became involved in something, the likes of which he had never experienced before. This was when Kim Chi had a baby only a few days after the wedding. Mr Bong's family was thrown into chaos. Bong got drunk and threw the bride out of the house. Tuan took a knife and stabbed at his father who fortuitously slipped over and avoided the attack. As she didn't have any way of keeping herself, my father had to take in his brother's daughter-in-law. My family had two extra mouths to feed. My wife didn't say anything. Miss Lai had more duties. It was fortunate that, as well as being simple, she also liked children.

Five

One night I was reading the Russian magazine, _Sputnik_, when my father came in quietly. 'I want to discuss something with you,' he said. I made some coffee which my father didn't drink. 'Have you been paying attention to what Thuy's been doing?' he asked. 'It gives me the creeps.'

The Maternity Hospital where my wife worked carried out abortions. Every day, she put the aborted foetuses into a Thermos flask and brought them home. Mr Co cooked them for the dogs and pigs. I had in fact known about this, but overlooked it as something of no importance. My father led me out to the kitchen and pointed to a pot full of mash in which there were small lumps of foetus. I kept silent. My father cried. He picked up the Thermos flask and hurled it at the pack of Alsatians: 'Vile! I don't need wealth that's made of this!' The dogs barked. My father went off up to the house. My wife came in and spoke to Mr Co: 'Why didn't you put it through the meat grinder? Why did you let Father see it?' Mr Co stammered: 'I forgot, I'm sorry, Aunt.'

In December, my wife called someone and sold the whole pack of Alsatians. She said: 'Stop smoking those imported Galang cigarettes. This year our income is down by 27,000 dong and our expenditure is up by 18,000, leaving us 45,000 out of pocket.'

Kim Chi recovered from the birth of the child and went to work. 'I'm grateful to everyone here,' she said, 'but now I must leave.' 'Where will you go?' I asked, for Tuan had been thrown into prison for being a hoodlum. Kim Chi took her child back to her parents' house. My father accompanied her and went as far as hiring a private taxi for the trip. He also took advantage of the occasion to spend the day with Kim Chi's father, the Deputy Department Chief.

He had just come back from a mission to India and gave my father a piece of printed silk and fifty grams of tiger balm. My father gave the silk to Miss Lai and the tiger balm to Mr Co.

—————————— *Six* ——————————

Before New Year's Day, Mr Co said to my wife and me: 'I wish to ask you both a favour.' 'What is it?' asked my wife. Mr Co broached the subject in a roundabout way. Basically, he wanted to visit his home village. While living with us for six years, he had made an effort to put some money aside, and, in accordance with custom, he wanted to go back to exhume his wife's remains and rebury them in a new grave. After so long away, he was sure the price of coffins would have fallen. 'Fidelity to the dead is our first duty,' he said, quoting an ancient aphorism. After living so long in the city, he also wanted to visit his village to make his relatives feel happy that he remembered them. He had been away a long time now, but even after it's been dead three years 'a fox looks back to the mountain'. My wife cut in: 'So when do you want to go?' Mr Co scratched his head: 'I want to go for ten days and return to Hanoi on the 23rd, before the New Year.' My wife made a calculation: 'All right. Thuan (Thuan is my name), do you think you can get some time off work?' 'I think so,' I said. Mr Co continued, 'We would like to invite your father to come with us for the trip,' he said. 'I don't like that idea. What would he say?' my wife responded. 'He's already agreed,' said Mr Co. 'Without him, I wouldn't have thought of moving my wife's grave.' 'How much money do you have?' inquired my wife. Mr Co replied: 'I have 3,000 dong, your father gave me

2,000, that makes 5,000.' My wife said: 'All right. Don't take the 2,000 from Father. I'll make it up and give you 5,000 more. That means the three of you will have 10,000. You'll be able to go.'

Before they left, my wife cooked a big dinner. The entire family, including Mr Co and Miss Lai, sat down to eat. Miss Lai was very happy, wearing a new dress that was made from the military material my father had given her when he returned home. Mi and Vi teased her: 'You're the prettiest, Lai.' Miss Lai laughed gently: 'No, I'm not. Your mother is the prettiest.' My wife said to her: 'When you go, make sure you look after my father-in-law on the trip.' My father said: 'Perhaps I shouldn't go?' Mr Co was concerned by this comment. 'Oh Dear,' he cried, 'I've already sent a telegram to say you're coming. It would tarnish your reputation.' My father sighed: 'What reputation have I got to lose?'

Seven

My father went to Thanh Hoa with Mr Co and Miss Lai on a Sunday morning. On the Monday night, I was watching television, when I heard a 'thump' and ran quickly outside to find that my mother had collapsed in a corner of the garden. She had been helpless for the last four years; she had to be fed and taken outside. Each day, Miss Lai had attended to her without any trouble. But this day, with Miss Lai gone, I had given her her meals, but forgotten to take her to the toilet. I helped my mother inside with her head slumped down on her chest. I couldn't see any sign of an injury. I stayed awake half the night watching her. Her body was very cold and her eyes were wild. I was afraid and called my wife. Thuy said: 'Mother is old.' Next day, my mother wouldn't eat. The day after that, she still wouldn't eat and made no attempt to go outside. I washed her underwear and changed her sleeping mat. Some days this happened a dozen times. I knew that Thuy and my two daughters couldn't stand filth, so I always washed and changed her clothes—not in the house, but down at the canal. She continued to bring up the medicine she took.

On the Saturday, my mother suddenly stood up. She went by herself for a stroll around the garden. She was able to eat. I said: 'That makes me happy.' My wife didn't say anything, and, that afternoon, I saw her put away ten metres of white cloth and heard her call the carpenter. 'Prepared, were you?' I asked. My wife replied: 'No.'

Two days later, my mother fell ill again. She rejected food and had to be helped out to the toilet as before. She went into a rapid decline, excreting a stinking thick brown liquid. I poured her some ginseng. My wife said: 'Don't give Mother any ginseng. It'll only make her worse.' I cried. It had been a very long time since I'd cried like that. My wife was silent, then she said: 'It's up to you.'

Mr Bong came over to visit. He said: 'The way she writhes around on the bed is terrible.' He then asked my mother: 'Hey there, do you recognize me, Sister?' My mother said: 'Yes.' 'So who am I?' Bong asked again. 'A person,' said my mother. Mr Bong cried out: 'So you care for me the most. The whole village treats me like a dog. My wife calls me an oaf. My son, Tuan, calls me a scoundrel. Only you call me a person.'

This was the first time I'd seen this ill-mannered, venturesome ox-cart driver turn into a child before my eyes.

Eight

My father returned home six hours after my mother died.
Mr Co and Miss Lai were distraught. 'It's our fault. If we'd
been at home, Grandmother wouldn't have died.'
'Nonsense,' said my wife. 'Oh Grandma,' Miss Lai cried,
'you've cheated me! Why didn't you let me look after you?'
Mr Bong laughed. 'You want to look after her, but you
went away. I'll close the coffin.' As he prepared my
mother's body for the shroud, my father cried and asked
Mr Bong: 'Why did she leave us so soon? Do all old people
die as wretchedly as this?' 'You don't know what you are
saying,' Mr Bong replied. 'Everyday, thousands of people in
our country die in shame and pain and sorrow. For you soldiers, its different: one shot—"bang"—that's a sweet way to
go.'

I had a temporary shelter built and told the carpenter to
make a coffin. Mr Co busied himself around the pile of
timber my wife had cut the day before. 'Are you afraid we'll
steal the wood?' the carpenter yelled out. Mr Bong asked:
'How thick are these boards?' 'Four centimetres,' I replied.
'What!' exclaimed Mr Bong. 'You could furnish a whole
lounge with this. When has anyone ever made a coffin with
such good wood? When you move the grave, make sure
you give me these boards.' My father sat silently and looked
deeply pained.

Mr Bong called out: 'Hey, Thuy, boil me a chicken and
cook me a pot of steamed rice.' 'How many measures of
rice, Uncle?' said my wife. 'Good heavens,' said Mr Bong,
'will you continue to speak so sweetly after today? Three
measures.' My wife turned to me and said: 'Oh, your relatives are dreadful.'

Mr Bong asked me: 'Who controls the finances in this
house?' 'My wife,' I answered. Mr Bong said: 'That's the

everyday expenses. I'm asking about who's looking after the funeral expenses.' 'My wife,' I answered. Mr Bong said: 'Good heavens, my boy! That can't be. She's of different flesh and blood. I'll speak to your father.' 'Let me,' I said. Mr Bong said: 'Give me 4,000. How many trays of food do you intend to serve at the funeral feast?' 'Ten trays,' I answered. 'That's not enough to touch the insides of the coffin bearers,' said Mr Bong. 'Go and talk to your wife. You need forty.' I gave him 4,000 dong and went into the house. My wife said: 'I've already heard. I'm counting on thirty trays at 800 dong each—three eights are twenty-four, 24,000. Other expenses, 6,000. I'll worry about getting the food. Miss Lai can arrange the banquet. Don't listen to Bong. He's an uncouth old man.' 'Mr Bong has already taken 4,000,' I said. 'You disappoint me so much,' complained my wife. 'I'll ask for it back, all right?' I said. 'Let it go,' she said. 'Regard it as a payment for his services. The old man's good enough, but he's poor.'

A traditional orchestra of four musicians arrived. My father went out to meet them just before my mother's body was placed in the coffin at four in the afternoon. Mr Bong pried her mouth open and placed nine dong inside it with a coin bearing the Emperor Khai Dinh's seal and an aluminium dime. 'To take you on the ferry,' he said. He then placed a pack of assorted playing cards inside the coffin: 'She always used to play cards,' Mr Bong added for good measure.

That night, I kept vigil over my mother's coffin, with my mind wandering in aimless thoughts. Death will come to us all, to each and every one of us.

Out in the courtyard, Mr Bong sat playing cards with the coffin bearers. Whenever he got a bad hand he ran in and bent low in prayer before my mother's coffin: 'I beg you, Sister, please help me clean out their pockets.'

My daughters Mi and Vi kept vigil with me. Mi asked: 'Why must you pay to go on death's ferry? And why put money in Grandmother's mouth?' Vi said: 'You have to keep it in your mouth to eat, don't you, Father?' 'You children don't understand,' I said through my tears. 'I don't understand either. It's a superstition.' Vi said: 'I understand. In life people don't know how much money they'll need. In death it's the same.'

I felt very lonely. So did my daughters. So did the whole crowd of gamblers. So did my father too.

Nine

It was only 500 metres in a direct line from my house to the cemetery, but the main path to it through the village gate ran for two kilometres. The path was too narrow for a hearse, and so the coffin had to be carried. Thirty bearers took it in turns to carry the coffin, many of whom I didn't know. They carried the coffin without any sense of the occasion, much as though they were carrying a house post. They chewed betel, smoked, and chatted as they went. When they rested, they stood and sat willy-nilly around the coffin. One of them stretched out on the ground and said with satisfaction: 'It's really cool. If we weren't so busy, I could nap here till nightfall.' Mr Bong urged them on: 'Hey there,' he said, 'let's get going, we've still got to get back for the banquet.'

So the procession moved on. Supported by a walking stick, I moved backwards in front of the coffin in accordance with the proper custom. Mr Bong said: 'When I die, my coffin bearers will all be gamblers, and pork won't be served at the funeral feast. Dog meat will.' 'Oh Brother, you are not joking at a time like this, are you?' my father said sadly. Mr Bong fell silent, then cried: 'Dear Sister! You've cheated me by going like this. . . . You've abandoned me. . . .' I thought 'Why cheat? Is it really possible for the dead to cheat the living? Is this cemetery full of cheats?'

After the burial everyone returned to the house. Twenty-eight trays of food had been placed out for the guests. As I looked at them, I was full of admiration for Miss Lai's work. Each table called out: 'Where's Miss Lai?' 'Here. . . . Here,' she twittered, running out with trays of wine and meat. When evening came, she had a bath and changed into fresh clothes. She went to the family altar and cried: 'Oh, Grandmother, please forgive me, for not being able to accompany you to your last resting place. . . . The other day you wanted to eat crab soup, but I was too lazy to cook it for you. When I go to the market, for whom can I buy food now? . . .' I felt very bitter. Thinking back over the previous ten years, I realized I'd never bought Mother a bread roll or a packet of sweets. Miss Lai cried: 'Would you be dead now, Grandmother, if I'd stayed at home?' My wife said: 'Stop crying.' 'Let her cry,' I retorted angrily. 'A funeral without the sound of sobbing would be very sad indeed. Who else in our family cries for Mother?' My wife did not seem to hear me and said: 'Thirty-two trays. Are you impressed by my exact calculations?' 'Exactly,' I answered.

'I'm going to have a look at the horoscope,' said Mr Bong. 'Your mother was not buried at an auspicious time. She will have "one change of grave, two funerals, one migration". Does she have a magic charm to ward off demons?' It was my father who answered: 'Magic charms are monkey business. In my life I've buried 3,000 people and not one of them with a magic charm.' Mr Bong said: 'They had a happy end: "bang", one shot.' He raised his index finger in the air and squeezed an imaginary trigger.

—————————————— *Ten* ——————————————

That New Year, my family neither bought any peach blossoms nor wrapped any rice cakes. On the afternoon of the second day, my father's old unit sent people to visit my mother's grave. They made a gift of 500 dong. Mr Chuong, a former deputy of my father's who had risen to the rank of General, went to the grave and lit incense. Captain Thanh, his aide, drew his pistol and fired three shots into the air. The children in the village would then spread the story that the army had fired a twenty-one gun salute on its visit to Madame Thuan's tomb. Anyway, after he had paid his respects, Mr Chuong asked my father: 'Would you like to come and visit your old unit? There'll be some manoeuvres in May, and we'll send a car for you.' 'Good,' said my father, 'I would like to come.'

Mr Chuong visited my family's estate and was guided around by Mr Co. 'Your estate is really something: a garden full of trees, a pond full of fish, pig pens, and a chicken coup, a country house. That certainly is reassuring for your retirement,' Mr Chuong said to my father. 'My son did it all,' replied my father. 'Your son's wife did it all,' I said. 'What about Miss Lai,' added my wife. Miss Lai smiled with embarrassment and nodded her head repeatedly as though she was having a fit. 'Not so,' she said. My father quipped: 'Thanks to her, we have a model household with gardens, ponds, and pens.'

On the third day, Kim Chi came in a pedicab to visit with her child. My wife gave her 1,000 dong for good luck in the New Year. 'Have you had any letters from Tuan?' inquired my father. 'No,' replied Kim Chi. 'It was all my fault,' he went on, 'I didn't know you were pregnant.' 'What's so unusual about that?' said my wife. 'These days, virgins don't exist. I work at the Maternity Hospital, I know.' Kim Chi was embarrassed. I cut in: 'Don't talk like that. These days, it really is difficult for a young girl to keep her virginity.' Kim Chi cried: 'Oh, Thuan, it's so shameful for us women. To give birth to a daughter tears me apart even more.' 'I've got two daughters too,' said my wife. 'So you think there's no shame in being a man, do you?' I asked. 'Men who have a heart feel shame,' said my father. 'The bigger the heart, the bigger the shame.' 'You all talk as though you've gone crazy,' said my wife. 'That's enough. Eat up. Kim Chi is with us today. I've treated everyone to steamed chicken with lotus hearts. That's what comes from my heart. Eating comes before everything else.'

_____ *Eleven* _____

Not far from our house there lived a young man named Con, whom the children called Confucius. He worked for a fish sauce company. But he also liked poetry and sent some of his poems to the prestigious journal *Literature and Art*. Con frequently came over to visit. He said: 'Surrealist poetry is the best.' He read me some poems by Lorca and Whitman. I didn't like Con and suspected that our friend visited for reasons that were more adventuresome than anything else. One day, I noticed my wife had a handwritten manuscript on the bed. 'They're Con's poems,' she said. 'Do you want to have a look at them?' I shook my head. 'You're getting old,' said my wife. An involuntary quiver flickered through my body.

One day I was busy at work and came home late. My father met me at the gate and said: 'Young Con has been over here since nightfall. He and your wife have been giggling in there, and he still hasn't gone. This is intolerable.'

'Go to bed, Father,' I said. 'What's the use of paying attention?' My father shook his head and went to his room. I pushed my motor bike out on to the road and sped aimlessly around the streets until it ran out of petrol. I pushed my bike to the corner of a park and sat down like a vagabond with nowhere to go. A girl with a powdered face walked passed and said: 'Hey, there, do you want to come with me?' I shook my head.

Con avoided me. Mr Co hated him and said to me one day: 'Why don't you just go and give him a hiding?' I almost nodded my head, but then thought, 'Leave it.'

I went to the library and borrowed a few books. Reading Lorca and Whitman I had the vague feeling that great artists are the loneliest people. Suddenly, I saw Con was right. I was just furious at him for being so ill-bred. Why didn't he give his poems to someone other than my wife to read?

My father said: 'You are weak. You put up with this because you can't live alone.' 'No, its not that. Life is full of jokes,' I said. 'So you think life is a farce?' asked my father. 'Not a farce,' I said, 'but it's not very serious either.' 'Why do I feel as though I'm lost?' my father muttered.

My Institute decided to send me down to the south to do some work. I said to my wife: 'It's OK if I go, isn't it?' 'No. Don't go,' she answered. 'Will you fix the bathroom door tomorrow?' she then asked. 'It's broken. The other day Mi was having a bath, and Con went through on some rotten pretext and scared her out of her wits. I've already barred the door to that vile fellow,' she explained, before bursting into tears. 'I really have failed you and the children,' she cried. I couldn't bear it and went out. If Vi had been there, she would have asked me: 'Hey, Father, they are crocodile tears, aren't they?'

Twelve

In May, my father's old unit sent a car to pick him up. Captain Thanh carried a letter from General Chuong. My father trembled as he opened it. It read: '... we very much hope you can come ... but only come if you are free, we won't press you.' I thought my father shouldn't go, but it was an awkward moment to say anything. My father had aged a great deal since he retired. But, holding the letter that day, he looked so young and sprightly. I was happy too. My wife prepared some food and clothes and said to put them into a travel-case. My father said: 'Put them in my pack.'

My father went out and said goodbye to everyone in the village, then went out to my mother's grave and told Captain Thanh to fire three shots into the air. That night he called Mr Co in to give him 2,000 dong and told him to have a tombstone engraved and sent back to Thanh Hoa to mark his wife's grave. Next, my father called Miss Lai in and said: 'Make sure you get married.' Miss Lai burst into tears: 'I'm so ugly, nobody will marry me. I'm also simple.' 'My dear child, don't you understand that simplicity gives us the strength to live,' said my father, choked with emotion. I didn't realize these words were an omen that he would not return from this trip.

Before he got into the car, my father took a small exercise book out of his pack and gave it to me. 'I've written a few things in here,' he said, 'take a look at them, my son.' Mi and Vi said goodbye to their grandfather. Mi asked: 'Are you going off to battle, Grandfather?' 'Yes,' he answered. Vi sang the first line of the song which went 'The road that leads to battle is very beautiful in this season', then added, 'isn't it, Grandfather?' 'You cheeky girl!' my father scolded affectionately.

_____ *Thirteen* _____

A few days after my father had left there was a hilarious incident at home. It happened that Mr Co and Mr Bong were
cleaning the mud out of the pond (my wife paid Mr Bong
200 dong a day and provided him food), when they suddenly saw the bottom of a water-jar that had risen to the
surface. The two men dug eagerly, then found another
water-jar. Mr Bong was sure that people in the old days had
used the jars to bury their jewellery. The two men told my
wife. Thuy went out and had a look and also waded into
the pond. Then Miss Lai, Mi, and Vi followed her. The
whole family was covered in mud. My wife had the pond
partitioned off and hired a Kholer water pump to empty it.
The atmosphere was very serious. Mr Bong was pleased
with himself, 'Since I saw it first, you'll have to divide the
booty up so that I get one jar.' After digging eagerly for a
day and turning up two cracked jars with nothing inside
them, Mr Bong said: 'There are sure to be more.'

The digging went on. Another jar was discovered. It was
also broken. The whole household was exhausted. With
everyone starving, my wife ordered some bread so that they
could regain their strength. The digging continued, and, at
a depth of almost ten metres they seized on a porcelain vase.
Everyone was overjoyed and thought that they had finally
struck gold. When they opened it, they found a string of
rusted bronze coins from the Bao Dai era and a pitted
medal. Mr Bong said: 'That's enough, I'm dead. I remember now. Many years ago, I robbed Han Tin's house with
that gangster, Nhan. We were chased away and Nhan threw
the vase into the pond.' Everyone burst out laughing. Nhan
had been a notorious thief on the outskirts of the city, and
Han Tin had joined the French colonial army. He had par-
ticipated in an anti-German movement during the First

World War known as the 'southern, silver spitting dragon campaign to expel the German rebels'. Both of them had been dead for ages. Mr Bong said: 'It doesn't matter, even if this whole village dies, I'll still have enough ferry money to stuff into their mouths.'

The next morning, I heard someone calling at the gate as I woke up. I went out and saw Con standing outside. 'The bastard,' I thought. 'There could be no worse omen for me than this vile lout.' Con said: 'Thuan, you have a telegram. Your father has died.'

Fourteen

The telegram was from General Chuong: 'Major-General Nguyen Thuan died while on duty at ... on.... He will be buried at the War Cemetery at ... on....' I was stunned. My wife made all the arrangements very quickly. I went out and hired a car and saw that everything was ready when I returned. 'Lock the house,' my wife said. 'Mr Co is staying behind.'

We took the most direct route to Cao Bang along Route One. But when we arrived, my father's funeral rites had been over for two hours.

'We owe your family an apology,' said General Chuong. 'Not at all. It was his destiny,' I replied. 'Your father was worthy of great honours,' emphasized General Chuong. 'So you buried him with military honours, did you?' I asked. 'Yes,' he replied. 'Thank you, Sir,' I said. General Chuong said: 'When your father was on the battlefield, he was always where the fighting was.' 'I know that,' I said, 'you don't have to tell me more.'

I cried like I had never cried before. I now knew what it was like to cry for the death of a father. It seemed to me that this was the biggest lament in the life of a human being.

My father's tomb was located in the war cemetery reserved for heroes. My wife brought a camera and took some photos. The next day, we took our leave, even though General Chuong wanted us to stay.

On the way back, my wife told me to drive slowly. For Mr Bong, it was his first car ride, and he liked it very much. 'Our country really is as pretty as a picture,' he said joyfully. 'Now I understand why we should love the country. Back at home, even though we live near the capital, I don't feel there's anything at all to love.' 'That's because you know it,' said my wife. 'Elsewhere people are the same; they then love Hanoi.'

'So around we go, turning like the figures on a magic lantern,' said Mr Bong. 'People here love it there, and people there love it here; put it all together and that's our country, our people. The homeland forever! The people forever! Hurrah for magic lanterns!'

Fifteen

Perhaps I should end my story here. After my father's death, the life of the family returned to what it had been before he retired. My wife went about her work as usual. I completed my electrolysis research. Mr Co grew quieter, partly because Miss Lai's condition worsened. In idle moments I read over the thoughts my father had noted in the exercise book he gave me before he departed. I feel I understand him better.

What I have written down is an account of the disordered events that took place in our lives during the year or so my father was in retirement. I regard these lines as the incense of incense sticks lit in remembrance of him. If anyone has had the heart to read them, I beg your pardon.

A Mother's Soul

WHEN Dang was two years old, his mother suddenly died from a serious illness. Therefore, the image he had of her was very vague. He lived with his maternal grandparents, and his father, who remarried, only came to visit him from time to time.

Meanwhile, Dang nurtured his image of his mother in a very particular way. His method was to question the efforts of those who looked after him. 'How would you do it, if you were my mother?' he would think to himself. When he had a bath and his grandmother scrubbed him with great care, for example, he immediately thought that, if his mother were bathing him, it wouldn't be like that. His mother would only wash his head and scrub the main parts, leaving the rest for him to wash. It was the same with eating: if his mother were feeding him, it would not have been the way his grandfather did. His grandfather did not understand that he did not like Chinese sausage. Instead, he always tried to force Dang to eat it, got angry when he refused, and, finally, ate the sausage himself. Dang didn't feel sorry about the sausage; he was just unhappy that his grandfather didn't understand him.

Now, when he was seven, Dang concluded that no one would ever be able to look after him as his mother would have done. It was a case of everyone doing either too much or too little for him, and just not hitting the mark. He had become a sad child who was too sensitive for his own good, and he did not know how to overcome this problem.

Until he was seven, he just hung around the house. All the people he lived with were grown-ups who did not understand him. Nor could they live up to his mother. That she was different was obvious. She was someone wonderful he could not actually visualize, but whose presence he certainly felt in all his self-pity.

Among Dang's young friends was Thu. She was seven years old and had a father and mother, brothers and sisters. Coming from such a regular family, Thu's thoughts and feelings were bound to be different from his.

She was spontaneous and carefree. She could go out to play without her mother telling her to be home by a certain time. It was different for Dang. He was restrained by a set of rules. His grandparents always took their responsibility seriously. Even for such a harmless thing as playing with Thu, they still kept a close check on him.

Thu had pink ears and black, flashing eyes. Dang did not know why, but he liked caressing those ears and looking deeply into those eyes.

'You look as though you've swallowed me. What did you find there?' Thu said to him one day.

Dang was bewildered. If he looked at his mother, he was sure that her eyes would be exactly like that.

'Nothing. I didn't find anything,' he said evasively. 'Tell me, do you cry easily?'

'Sometimes,' replied Thu. 'But I've got to have something to cry for. Nobody cries for nothing.'

'But I sometimes cry for nothing,' Dang said, and tried to think when he had done this.

'That's your mother's soul,' Thu said seriously. She had heard stories of people calling back the souls of the departed. 'Your mother's soul comes to you and says: "Dang, go ahead and cry, cry to release your sadness." '

'What is sadness?' asked Dang.

'I don't know, but it's like losing something. Yesterday I lost a hairpin, so I was sad.'

'If I lose something, I'm not sad,' Dang said bravely. 'My grandfather said: "People lose very many things in their lives. They lose their wealth, their souls." '

'What is a soul?'

'It's in here,' Dang pointed to his belly.

'People's bellies are full of dung,' Thu said, shivering all over. 'My mother said that. If it's true, it's terrible, isn't it?'

'That's just your mother talking loosely,' Dang reassured her. 'My grandfather says peoples' souls are like violin strings: when the wind blows across them they vibrate gently: a–a–a–a. . . .'

'A soul that cries a–a is really clever,' Thu laughed lightly. She closed her eyes and mimicked the sound: 'a–a–a–a'.

'You don't understand at all,' Dang said, displeased. 'You haven't got a soul. You are like your mother. All your mother likes is money.'

'That is true,' Thu admitted. 'Perhaps my mother really doesn't have a soul! Perhaps she doesn't need one! And what's the use of it? If it cries a–a when the wind blows across it, it's very frightening!' Thu again laughed lightly.

Dang knitted his brows. He didn't like Thu teasing him. 'That's enough of you laughing at me like that,' he said. 'Girls who laugh a lot are not very charming.'

'What does it matter if you lack charm?'

'If you lack charm, you won't find a husband.'

'You devil. You're talking like an old man!' Thu became angry. She wanted revenge: 'You are an orphan, you are very cruel.'

Dang was shocked by these remarks. His face went white.

Thu had stuck the point of the needle into the spot where it hurt most. Tears scalded his cheeks, his lips trembled. The way the colour of his face changed alarmed her.

'Now now, I was only joking. You cry too easily. That's enough, if you want me to have a soul, then I'll have one.' Thu was uneasy, and she began to invent stories to coax him along. 'That's right,' she said. 'Last night I heard a very soft sound coming from somewhere: u-u-u-u. I didn't know what it was. It sounded like the wind blowing across the gables. Do you think that could have been the sound of my soul?'

Dang listened and, perceiving the troubled look on Thu's face, knew she was making up the story. He felt offended. He howled. Thu burst into tears. Then, when she heard the howling, Dang's grandmother ran out, scowling angrily at Thu. She swung her arm and slapped young Thu hard on her fair, white cheek. Dang took a peek and did not know why the red blotches on Thu's cheek made him think of the petals of a flower.

In first grade, Dang and Thu sat together at the same desk, and he always felt that, in many ways, his ability to adapt to the world around them was inferior to hers. She got on more easily with their schoolfriends than he did. With their studies it was the same: she was quicker than he was. Without realizing it, Dang felt a certain dependence on his friend. In a way that she was not aware of, Thu was like a spiritual support for Dang. She protected him from his enemies in the class; she prompted him when he was writing his compositions. Sometimes, it was even as though Thu took advantage of her role with Dang. Their classmates mocked them: 'Thu is the mother, Dang is the child! Dang has to ask his mother for everything!'

At first, such jeering made Dang furious. Later, he became accustomed to it, partly because of his passive nature. Gradually, he even developed a special kind of respect for Thu that is usually reserved for adults. She was very proud of her role and said to him: 'I'm your mother! It's true! What they say is right!'

Dang laughed uneasily: he did not believe Thu could become a mother. However, he did not answer back. He actually needed a mother, and didn't his grandfather say, 'Every woman has a mother's nature.' Could Thu become a mother?

A little later, the following events occurred.

Their lady teacher organized an out-of-town camp for the class, and Dang and Thu got lost. Night fell quickly over the rice fields, where the low bushes steadily disappeared into the darkness, and the white phosphorous lights of the dragon-flies blinked on and off. Thu cried; she regretted that it had been her idea to wander off so far.

'Be quiet! Crying doesn't do any good,' Dang scolded. Then he sighed: 'I'm so hungry! Do you have anything to eat?'

'No, I haven't,' Thu replied, 'I feel hungry too.'

'If you were a mother, you'd have prepared everything for the journey. At least you'd have some food,' Dang joked with purposeful cruelty. 'You don't feel any responsibility for me at all. Go on, cry again. You're a rotten mother!'

Thu was furious. But, searching through her pockets, she victoriously came up with a candy.

'I've got a candy! That's right, last night Aunty Hai gave me a candy and I forgot all about it.' Thu had regained the initiative and was calm again. 'Actually,' she said, 'I didn't forget at all. I brought it along for the trip, then I purposely put it out of my mind.'

Dang was doubtful. He snatched the candy and took a bite of it. Yes, it certainly was a candy—and a lemon one too. So could it be that Thu was a real mother? Mothers can always find something in emergencies. He bit off half the candy, gave the other half to Thu and, as he used the tip of his tongue to roll the candy around his mouth, he began to think.

'It would be good if we had a fire,' he began with one of his searching jokes. 'If you are a mother, what will you do?'

Thu was perplexed. She wouldn't be able to find any matches even if she did turn her pockets out. Luck could only come once in the form of a candy. She wrinkled her eyes and thought.

'Come on, let's go. There'll be a fire up ahead. I'll find a fire.'

Dang smiled sadly and said in a doubtful tone: 'If you find a fire, then you really are a mother.' He laughed: 'And if you find a fire, I'll think of a way to signal the others so they can come and find us.'

They moved along the edge of the fields, talking. They went into a vacant piece of land that contained a number of dark, deserted mounds: it was a cemetery. Thu suddenly remembered how, in the previous year, she had gone back with her Aunt Hai to her home village to refurbish their ancestral graves. It had been a graveyard like this. They had lit incense after attending to the graves and thrown the matches away.

Dang whispered: 'Are you afraid? I am. . . .'

'Don't be afraid,' Thu said nervously. 'You and I will go and look around that new grave over there. That's where the fire will be.'

They went over to the freshly attended grave. There were fresh flowers all around it, and many incense sticks had recently been lit there too.

'Here we are!' Thu cried out. She had found an old box of matches with a dozen matches in it.

In their excitement the two children forgot their fear. Dang was full of admiration for her. 'You're a genius,' he said. 'Why did you think there would be matches here?'

Thu laughed. She was now a mother. And mothers had the right to keep their secrets from their children. 'You don't understand anything,' she said proudly. 'I found it because I'm a mother.'

Dang gathered some firewood. He covered the matchbox with his shirt to dry the moisture out of it. Then, he lit the fire. About half an hour later the teacher found the two children.

Because this was a children's story, the grown-ups needed no explanation for it. Smitten by harsh reality, they could not appreciate its wonderful significance. For Dang his story was like a marvellous fairy-tale that his elders could never understand.

But his grandparents still spoilt him. He was a precious possession of theirs. They usually laid the blame for his bad habits on Thu. His obstinacy, his habit of making fun of people, his lazy neglect, even his slow learning: all of this they blamed on his friend. Dang knew his grandparents were wrong. The older he got, the more stubborn and lonely he became, and it was with increasing sensitivity that he responded to his fate as an orphan.

One day he smashed a figurine of Ong Phuc, the Lord of Happiness. His grandmother bewailed this broken icon: 'Clumsy fool,' she scolded, 'it's all because of that brat Thu.'

Tears streamed down his cheeks; he felt both indignant and hurt. He ran down to the kitchen where he sat in a dark corner. Here he sobbed violently, while his grandmother howled madly in the house. He could hear the sound of an electric tramcar hurtling down the street. Suddenly, thoughts of death flashed through his mind. That's the answer! Fall on the tracks! A great mass of steel would pass over him and that would be the end. There was nothing to do, nothing to think about. In ten minutes, another tramcar would pass by. The thing he needed most was to inform Thu. She was his good friend. She could explain death to him. What meaning did the Lord of Happiness have? Happiness, Good fortune, Longevity: what meaning did they have? Dang slipped out the door and ran down the street. The electric tramcar was 300 metres away. Thu stood on the roadside.

'Why are you doing that?' Thu screamed and stared in horror.

Dang floundered. His face was drained of its colour. The tramcar glided past. 'Oh Good Heavens! ...' Thu pushed Dang out of the way. He fell heavily and passed out.

Dang did not die. Thu had saved him, but in doing so her legs had been broken by the tramcar. The two children were taken to hospital. Dang had a high fever and tossed in his bed throughout the night.

'Mother ... Mother ... Mother. ...'

The sound of the word 'mother' was like the sound of the wind blowing across the gables.

In a dream Dang saw himself standing with Thu on a high place. Looking down from their vantage point, people and cars seemed infinitesimally small. The wind howled. Thu laughed lightly, revealing her shiny white teeth. 'Hey, Dang!' she called, 'I'll rise into the air with these legs!' She held out her naked legs in front of his eyes. 'I'll fly, as if in a fairy-tale. . . .'

So saying, Thu left him. She stepped off into the heavens with her arms parting the air. Dang pressed his chest against the veranda rail, chilled by the sharp awareness that he was a lonely orphan.

He called to Thu: 'Wait! Wait for me to come with you! First tell me how to fly like that! First tell me how to fly like that!' Thu glided on. 'You can't fly like me! Don't you understand? It's because I'm a mother!'

Dang woke up with a start. The dream faded. He opened his eyes and looked carefully around the hospital room. Beside Dang, his grandparents watched him attentively. Suddenly, he trembled, because he could see the eyes of his grandparents looking straight through him.

Dang looked out through the window. The sky was deep-blue. A wire clothes line shook gently in a light breeze. And if you had very sharp hearing, you could have heard a faint vibration: 'u-u-u-u. . . .'

Salt of the Jungle

A month after the new year is the best time to be in the jungle. The vegetation is bursting with fresh buds, and its leaves are deep-green and moist. Nature is both daunting and delicate, and this is due, in large measure, to the showers of spring rain.

At around this time, your feet sink into carpets of rotting leaves, you inhale pure air, and, sometimes, your body shudders with pleasure, because a drop of water has fallen from a leaf and struck your bare shoulder. Miraculously, the vexations of your daily life can be completely forgotten, because a small squirrel has sprung on to a branch. And, as it happened, it was at just such a time that Mr Dieu went hunting.

The idea to go hunting had come to him when his son, who was studying in a foreign country, sent him a gift of a double-barrelled shotgun. The gun was as light as a toy, and so sleek that he could not have dreamt such a beautiful thing existed. Mr Dieu was sixty, and, at that age, both a new shotgun and a spring day for the hunt really made life worth living.

To dress for the occasion, he put on a warm quilted coat and trousers, a fur hat, and laced up a pair of high boots. To be well prepared, he also took a ration of glutinous rice rolled up into a ball the size of his fist. He moved up along the bed of a dry stream towards its source, a mile from which was the fabled kingdom of limestone caves.

Mr Dieu turned on to a beaten track that wound through the jungle. As he moved along this track, he was aware that the trees on either side of it were full of blue birds. Yet, he did not shoot. With a gun like his, it would have been a waste of ammunition, especially when he had already had his fill of blue birds. They were tasty enough, but had a fishy flavour. In any case, he had no need to shoot birds with a loft full of pigeons at home.

At a turn in the track, Mr Dieu was startled by a rustling noise in a bush. A clump of motley vines flew up in front of his face, and, as he caught his breath, a pair of jungle fowls shot out in front of the bush with their heads down, clucking. Mr Dieu raised his shotgun and aimed. However, the fowls did not present a good target. 'I'll miss,' he thought. He considered the situation, and sat down motionless in the same position for a very long time, waiting for the jungle to become quiet again. The fowls would think there was nobody there: it would be better that way—for them, and for him.

The mountain range was full of towering peaks. Mr Dieu looked at them as he contemplated his strength. To bag a monkey or a mountain goat would certainly be something. But he knew that mountain goats were difficult game. It was only by some stroke of luck that he would get a good shot at one, and he did not think that luck would come.

As he weighed carefully the pros and cons, Mr Dieu decided to move along the foot of the limestone mountain range and hunt monkeys in the Dau Da forest. He would be surer of finding food and wasting less energy. Mount Hoa Qua and Thuy Liem Cave were along the valley and, like the forest, they were legendary monkey haunts. Mr Dieu also knew that he did not have difficulty shooting monkeys.

He stopped on a piece of rising ground, amid trees

covered with climbing vines. This species of tree was unknown to him, with its silver leaves and golden flowers like ear-rings that hung down to the earth. Mr Dieu sat quietly and observed, for he wanted to see if there were any monkeys there. These animals are as crafty as human beings; when they gather food they always put out sentries, and monkey sentries are very acute. If you don't see them, there is no hope for the hunt, no hope of hitting the leader of the troop. Of course, the leader was only a monkey. But it was not just any monkey. It would be the one that fate had singled out for him. So he had to wait, had to be cunning if he wanted to shoot his monkey.

Mr Dieu sat quietly and relaxed for half an hour. The spring weather was warm and silky. It had been a long time since he had had the opportunity to sit as peacefully as this. And as he sat without a care in the world, the tranquillity of the jungle flowed through his being.

Suddenly, a swishing sound came rushing from out of the Dau Da Forest. It was the sound of a large animal moving through the trees. Mr Dieu knew it was the leader of a monkey troop. He also knew that this monkey was formidable. It would appear with the brutal self-confidence of a king. Mr Dieu smiled and watched carefully.

The sound continued a while; then, suddenly, the beast appeared. It rapidly propelled itself through the jungle as though it never rested. Mr Dieu admired its nimbleness. However, it disappeared in a flash, leaving him with a sharp stab of disappointment that this king-like creature would not be his. The elation he had felt since leaving home that morning was beginning to subside.

As soon as the leader disappeared, a gaggle of about twenty monkeys swung into view, criss-crossing Mr Dieu's field of vision from very many angles. Some of them appeared on perches high up in the trees, others swung through the branches, and still others sprang to the ground. Within this medley of movement, Mr Dieu noticed three monkeys that stayed together: a male, a female, and their young baby. He knew immediately that the male monkey was his prey.

Mr Dieu felt hot. He took off his hat and quilted coat and placed them under a bush. He also placed his ball of glutinous rice there. Gradually, he moved into a depression in the ground. He observed carefully, and noticed that the female monkey was standing guard. That was convenient, for with a becoming sense of female vanity, she had distracted herself with the task of picking off her body lice.

Mr Dieu made his calculations, then crept along keeping windward of the female monkey. He had to get within 20 metres of the troop before he would be able to shoot. He crawled rapidly and skilfully. Once he had located his prey, he was sure he would kill it. That monkey was his. He was so certain of this, he even felt that if he stumbled or made a careless move it would not make any difference.

Yet, even though he thought like this, Mr Dieu still stalked the monkey troop carefully. He knew that nature was full of surprises, that one could never be too cautious.

He rested the shotgun in the fork of a tree, while the family trio had no inkling that disaster was near. The father was perched in a tree plucking fruit and throwing it down to the mother and child. Before he threw it, he always selected the best fruit and ate it himself. 'How contemptible,' thought Mr Dieu as he squeezed the trigger. The shotgun blast stunned the monkey troop for several seconds: the male monkey had fallen heavily to the ground with its arms outstretched.

The confusion into which the shotgun blast had thrown the monkey troop caused Mr Dieu to tremble. He had done something cruel. His arms and legs went limp, with the kind of sensation that overcomes someone who has just overexerted himself with heavy work, and the troop disappeared into the jungle before he knew it. The female monkey and the baby also ran off after the others, but, after moving some distance, the female suddenly turned around and returned. Her mate, whose shoulder had been shattered by the shotgun pellets, was trying to raise himself but kept falling back on to the ground.

The female monkey advanced carefully to where her mate had fallen and looked around, suspicious of the silence. The male monkey let out a pitiful scream, before he became silent again and listened, with a frantic expression on his face.

'Oh, get away from there!' Mr Dieu groaned softly. But the female monkey looked as though she was prepared to sacrifice herself. She went up to her mate and lifted him up in her arms. Mr Dieu angrily raised his shotgun. Her readiness to sacrifice herself made him hate her like some bourgeois madame who paraded her noble nature. He knew all about the deceptions in which such theatrical performances were rooted; she could not deceive an old hunter like him.

As Mr Dieu prepared to squeeze the trigger, the female monkey turned around and looked at him with terror in her eyes. She threw down the male monkey with a thud and fled. Mr Dieu breathed a sigh of relief, then laughed quietly. He rose to his feet and left his hiding-place.

'I've made a mistake!' Mr Dieu cursed under his breath. For when he moved from his hiding-place, the female monkey immediately turned around. 'She knows I'm human,' he sighed, 'the game is up.' Exactly so, the female monkey now kept him in the corner of her eye as she rushed headlong back to her mate. She deftly put her arms around him and hugged him to her chest. The two rolled around in a ball on the ground. She was acting like a crazy old woman. She was going to sacrifice herself recklessly, because of some noble instinct that nature prized. This stirred deep feelings of guilt in Mr Dieu's heart. He had revealed himself as an assassin, while the female monkey, who faced death, still bared her teeth in a smile. Whatever he did now, he could only suffer, he could never rest, and he could even die two years before his time if he shot the female monkey at this moment. And all of this was because he had come out of his hiding-place two minutes too soon.

As if to torment him, the monkeys took each other by the hand and ran off. 'You pathetic old figure, Dieu,' he thought sadly, 'with a pair of arthritic legs like yours, how are you going to run as fast as a monkey driven by loyalty and devotion?' The female monkey waved her bow legs, grinned, and made obscene gestures. Mr Dieu angrily hurled his shotgun down in front of him. He wanted to frighten the female monkey into releasing her mate.

At the moment the shotgun hit the ground, the baby monkey suddenly appeared from a rocky mound. It grabbed the sling of the shotgun and dragged it off along the ground. The three monkeys scurried off on all fours, shrieking. Mr Dieu was struck dumb for a second, then burst out laughing: his predicament was so ridiculous.

He picked up a handful of dirt and stones and threw it at the monkeys, as he took off howling in pursuit. The monkeys, who were terrified by these developments, split up with the two adults veering off in the direction of the mountains and the baby running towards the cliff. 'Losing the shotgun will be disastrous,' thought Mr Dieu, and he continued to chase the baby monkey. He charged forward and narrowed the distance between them to the extent that only a jagged rock prevented him from reaching his gun.

By chasing the baby monkey, Mr Dieu had taken a course of action which had extraordinary consequences.

These began when the small monkey just rolled over the edge of the precipice, holding the shotgun sling tightly. Evidently, it was too inexperienced to react in any other way.

Mr Dieu was pale and soaked with sweat. He stood looking down over the cliff with his body shaking. From far below came the echo of a piercing scream, the likes of which he had never heard before. He drew back in fear, as a mist swirled up from the abyss and enveloped the vegetation around him. Very quickly the entire landscape was obscured by eerie vapours. He ran back to the mountain. It was perhaps the first time since his childhood that Mr Dieu had run as though he was being chased by a ghost.

Mr Dieu was exhausted when he reached the foot of the mountain. He sat down on the ground, looking back in the direction of the precipice which the mist had now obscured. He remembered suddenly that this was the most feared place in the valley: the place that hunters called Death Hollow. Here, with alarming regularity, somebody perished in the mist each year.

'Ghosts?' thought Mr Dieu. 'Forsaken spirits usually take the form of white monkeys, don't they?' It had been a white monkey that seized the gun. Moreover, this had been such an extraordinary action that Mr Dieu began to wonder if what he had been chasing was really the monkey that simple appearances suggested.

'Am I dreaming?' he wondered, looking around. 'Is all of this happening?' He stood up and looked at the mountain wall on the other side of Death Hollow. He was stunned, for, now, without a trace of mist, the dome of the sky was clear and vast, and the entire landscape was visible in every detail.

An agitated cry came from somewhere above him. Mr Dieu looked up, and there he saw the wounded monkey lying across a rock ledge. The female monkey was nowhere to be seen, and so, very happy in the certainty that he would now catch his monkey, Mr Dieu searched for a way to climb up to the rock ledge.

Finding a way up the side of the steep, slippery mountain was both difficult and dangerous. Mr Dieu gauged his strength. 'Whatever way, I'm going to get that monkey,' he murmured to himself, as he calmly used the crevices in the rock-face to work his way up.

After about ten minutes, Mr Dieu felt hot. He chose a spot where he could stand, and took off his boots and outer garments and placed them in the fork of a mulberry tree. He climbed on quickly with no doubts about his strength to reach the ledge.

The slab of rock on which the wounded monkey lay was smooth and seemed somewhat unstable. Beneath it, there was a crevice as wide as Mr Dieu's hand, which would allow him to pull himself up. He shuddered, for he was frightened by the feeling the slab gave him that it might move and roll down the mountain at any moment. Nature was cruel and might want to test his courage further.

Mr Dieu finally pulled himself up on to the rock ledge with his elbows, and there he saw an extremely beautiful monkey with fine golden hair. It lay prone with its hands raking across the surface of the rock, as though it was trying to pull itself along. Its shoulder was stained red with blood.

Mr Dieu put his hand on the monkey and felt its feverish body heat. 'Easier than putting a hand on a sparrow,' he thought. Next, he slipped his hand under the monkey's chest and lifted it to estimate its weight. However, he withdrew his hand quickly when the chest emitted the sound of a low, but very disconcerting 'hum', which made him feel that his intervention had aroused Death's fury. The monkey stirred Mr Dieu's pity when it trembled and rolled its sluggish eyes towards him. The shotgun pellets had smashed the monkey's shoulder blade and come out through four centimetres of bone. Each time the bones rubbed together, the monkey writhed in pain.

'I can't leave you like that,' said Mr Dieu. He picked some Lao grass, crumpled it in his hand, and put it in the monkey's mouth. The monkey chewed the grass carefully, while Mr Dieu applied a handful of leaves to its wound to stem the bleeding. The monkey curled its body into a ball and again turned its moist eyes towards Mr Dieu. The old man looked away.

The monkey then buried its head in Mr Dieu's arms, and a stammering sound came out of its mouth. The monkey was like a helpless child imploring him for help. Mr Dieu felt very miserable. 'It is better for me if you resist,' he murmured, looking down at the suffering brow of the shrivelled monkey. 'I am old, and you know the sympathy of old people is easily aroused. What can I use to bandage you, poor monkey?'

Mr Dieu considered the situation. He had no choice but to take off his underpants and use them to bandage the monkey's wound. When he did this, the bleeding stopped and the monkey no longer groaned.

Naked now, Mr Dieu picked the monkey up and kept adjusting its weight in his arms as he found his way back down the mountain. Then, suddenly, as though impelled by some force, the mountainside began to slide away with a tremendous roar from about half way up.

An avalanche!

Mr Dieu jumped in terror and clung tightly to a rock. A section of the path he had taken to come up the mountain now flashed down past him, leaving only the surface of the rock-face shorn smooth. Mr Dieu could no longer see the mulberry tree where he had left his boots and outer garments. To descend that way was now impossible. He would have to circle around behind the mountain. Even though it was further this way, it was the only safe alternative.

Mr Dieu groped his way down the mountain for more than two hours before he reached the bottom. He had never had as difficult and as exhausting an ordeal as that. His body was covered in scratches. The monkey hovered between life and death, as he dragged it along the ground. For Mr Dieu, it was agonizing to have to drag the monkey like that, but he no longer had the strength to carry it in his arms.

When Mr Dieu reached the clump of bushes and vines he had hidden behind that morning, he stopped to pick up his hat and coat and the ball of glutinous rice he had left there. But, to his astonishment, he found that a termites' nest as tall as rice stubble had risen in that spot. The nest was a sticky mound of fresh red earth plastered together with termites' wings. Unfortunately, his things had been mixed up in the nest and turned to mash! Mr Dieu sighed, turned around in frustration, and lifted the monkey up in his arms. 'How humiliating it will be to return home naked,' he scowled angrily. 'I'll become a laughing stock.'

He set off, thinking about what he was going to do, as he walked around in a circle until he found the track again. 'How did this happen?' he burst out laughing. 'Who's ever shot a monkey like this? A sparrow and a half of meat on it. Golden hair like dye. You shoot an animal like this even though you've got no clothes! Serves you right, you old fool!'

There was a faint sound of something moving behind him. He gave a start, turned around, and recognized the female monkey who immediately disappeared behind a bush. It turned out that she had followed Mr Dieu from the mountain without him realizing it. He felt this was weird.

After moving on for some distance, Mr Dieu turned around again and, to his exasperation, saw that she was still following him. He put the male monkey down on the ground, gathered some stones, and chased the female monkey away. She gave a high-pitched scream and disappeared. When Mr Dieu looked around a little later, she still tagged along behind him.

The trio continued to plod on through the jungle. The female monkey was incredibly persistent, and made Mr Dieu feel that it was all so terribly unfair, that he was being pursued by misfortune.

By now, the male monkey had also recognized the call of his mate. He wriggled around. This wriggling made Mr Dieu feel extremely wretched, and it so exhausted him that he didn't have the strength to carry the monkey any further. To make matters worse, the monkey's hands clawed at Mr Dieu's chest and made it bleed. Mr Dieu could no longer bear the situation, and, in a fury, he threw the monkey down on the ground.

As the monkey lay sprawled out on a piece of wet grass, Mr Dieu sat down and looked at it. Not far away, the female monkey bobbed out from behind the foot of a tree to see what was happening. As Mr Dieu now looked at both of the monkeys, he felt a burning sensation on the bridge of his nose. Profoundly sad, he was overcome by the realization that, in life, responsibility weighs heavily on every living thing.

'All right, I'll set you free,' declared Mr Dieu. He sat peacefully for a moment, then stood up without warning, and spat a wad of saliva on the ground near his feet. After hesitating for some time, he finally hurried off. The female monkey shot straight out of her hiding-place as though she had been waiting for exactly this moment, and ran quickly to her mate.

Mr Dieu turned on to another track because he wanted to avoid people. This track was choked with bramble bushes that made the going difficult, but they were covered by masses of *tu huyen* flowers. Mr Dieu stopped in amazement. *Tu huyen* flowers only bloom once in thirty years, and people that come across them are said to meet with good luck. The flowers are white. They are as small as the head of a toothpick, and have a salty taste. People call them 'salt of the jungle'. When the jungle is braided together with these flowers, it is a sign that the country is blessed with peace and abundant harvests.

When he came out of the valley, Mr Dieu went down into the fields. The spring rain was gentle but very good for the rice seeds. Naked and lonely, he went on his way. A little later, his shadow faded into the curtain of rain.

In only a few days it would be the beginning of summer. The weather would gradually get warmer ...

Lessons from the Country

My mother is a peasant,
and I am a child of the country.
The Narrator

WHEN I completed high school in the year I turned seventeen, I spent the summer holidays at the house of a classmate of mine. His name was Lam, and he lived at Nhai Hamlet, in Tach Dao Village, N Province.

Nhai Hamlet is located along the Canh River. This is a small river, and, in the dry season, a man can wade across it with the water only coming up to his chest in the deepest part. Lam's house was at one end of the hamlet, a long way down a narrow path. It was fenced off by spurge hedgerows. The roof was thatched with rice stubble, and the walls were made of cob. Three rooms with two open living areas under the gables on either side of the house made up the typical country dwelling. There was little furniture: a large box full of unhusked rice in the main room, two bamboo beds on either side. Clothes hung from wooden beams fixed along the walls. The sole decoration in the house was an old silk painting of the Lords of Happiness, Good Fortune, and Longevity. They were surrounded by a group of children offering peaches in their hands. Cobwebs stretched across the glass in the picture frame; fly dirt speckled its dull surface.

Lam's family was not large. There was his old grandmother, and his father and mother who worked in the fields. His elder brother had joined the army, and this brother's new wife, Hien, had only been in the family for six months. Lam had two younger siblings: his sister Khanh who was thirteen, and his little brother Tien who was four.

My own family lived in the city where my father was a teacher. My mother, who came from an old feudal family, stayed at home to 'lend support' to my father. My parents wanted me to go on with my studies. 'With an education you will be shielded from misfortune': that is what my mother said. Anyway, with only rare opportunities to visit the countryside, I certainly welcomed the chance I had now.

This was the first time I had travelled such a long way from home. My mother had said to Lam: 'He's still young, please look after him for me.' I saw Lam smile; although he was bigger than I was, he was four months younger.

Lam's family welcomed me warmly. Hien prepared two trays of food. One was carried out on to the veranda for Lam, his father, and me; the other was set out in the court-yard for Lam's grandmother, mother, and Hien, along with Khanh and little Tien. There were delicious servings of crab and vegetable soup, marinated eggplant, roasted prawns. To our tray were added some peanuts and two green guavas for Lam's father to eat as he drank his rice wine.

'Would you like to start gentlemen,' invited Hien. 'I want to be a gentleman too!' announced little Tien. 'Be quiet you naughty boy!' Lam's mother scolded. 'With a dicky bird no bigger than a chilli, how can you be a gentleman?' Khanh covered her mouth with her hand and laughed. I went red. Old Grandmother Lam sighed: 'Ah yes. . . . Gentlemen have all got big dicky birds.' Everyone rolled around laughing, except Lam's father whose tanned face had been deeply lined by hard work and simply suggested peaceful indifference. Young Tien started to cry. Hien tried to coax him along: 'Don't cry,' she said. 'Here, I'll give you this crab claw.' 'U ... u ... it's too small,' blubbered Tien, shaking his head. 'Well then,' said Hien, 'will you be happy if I buy you a pack of cards when I go to market tomorrow?' 'Gambling will be the end of him,' interjected Lam's mother. 'Don't buy him cards, or he'll be ruined by the time he grows up. Buy a whip for him!' 'I want some cards!' blubbered Tien. 'All right,' said Hien, winking at Lam's mother, 'I'll buy you the cards.' Grandmother Lam cut in: 'In the old days there was a ferry man, Mr Hai Chep, who was obsessed with gambling. First he lost his money, then he lost his land, his house, and his wife who finished up leaving him. So at night he would sit on his boat and cry. Both angry with life and full of remorse, he took a knife, cut off his balls, and threw them into the river. His wife didn't come back after that.' 'That's a cruel woman for you!' commented Lam's mother. 'What do you mean?' asked Grandmother Lam. 'What good could she do for him when he'd already cut off his balls and lost his prized possessions?' 'Terrible,' laughed Hien. 'That's a hair-raising story of yours, Grandmother!'

With all the excitement, the lunch seemed to end quickly. 'Hieu, have you had enough to eat?' Hien asked me, as Khanh scraped the pot clean. 'I've eaten four bowls,' I said, 'in Hanoi I usually eat only three.' 'Four bowls is not enough for a strong young man like you,' insisted Lam's mother. 'It takes nine bowls to fill up my husband. Even me, it takes six bowls before I've had enough.' Hien said: 'You've got a better appetite than I have, Mother, three bowls is all I can eat.' 'Go on, eat up!' Grandmother Lam urged me. 'The men won't look after you. When they eat, they sit above us up there on the veranda, and when they sleep they lie on top of us.' 'Don't you think that's enough, old woman!' scowled Lam's father. 'Enough yourself!' mumbled Grandmother Lam. 'I'm eighty, do you think I'm going to conceal the truth at my age?'

In the afternoon Lam's father suggested that he take Lam and me to fly a kite. Lam's mother said to his father: 'Actually, there are a few baskets of paddy I was going to ask you to husk for me.' 'Let Father go,' said Hien. 'I'll husk the paddy for you. It's not every day we have a guest.' Lam's father took down a kite that was as big as a basket-boat from inside the roof of the kitchen. It was covered with strong layers of papyrus, and a roll of rattan cord as thick as my index finger was attached to it. Lam took some sand to polish the three brass flutes that were fixed on to the kite so that they would glitter in the sky. At the same time, Lam's father softened the roll of rattan cord by soaking it in the pond. We waited for the late afternoon sun before we went out into the fields. With most of the fields harvested, we looked out across rice stubble to where fiery clouds whirled on the horizon. The deep odour of the earth emanated from the cracks in its surface. Some children from the hamlet ran out noisily after us. A couple of old men who were still sunning themselves on the edge of a pond forgot what they were doing and stood up to observe us. 'Old Ba Dinh is enjoying himself as usual,' someone remarked. 'There's a good wind today,' said someone else. 'The sound of the flutes will be good.'

Lam's father was naked from the waist up. Dressed only in a pair of shorts, his torso rippled with muscles. He carried the enormous roll of rattan over his shoulder, while Lam and I plodded along carrying the huge kite. 'We'll fly it from the high ground at Dam Tien,' Lam's father told us. 'You stand there and watch,' Lam directed me when we arrived. On reaching the highest point, Lam tested the wind and, with his hands, he pushed the kite up high into it. He looked like someone dancing.

I ran after Lam's father who was moving across the fields in an effort to pull the kite into the wind. He leant back as he ran, pulling strongly on the cord. The kite tilted and slid down through an arc in the air. Lam's father ran to the left. Cutting back up across its first arc, the kite carved another groove in the air. For a moment, it bounced lightly in the wind, before filling and rising straight up into the sky. Lam's father let out the roll of rattan cord. Beads of sweat glistened on his naked back. He panted as he ran, tumbled over, then ran and tumbled over again.

I ran on, out of breath, trying to keep up with Lam's father. He crossed half-harvested fields and waded through ditches. He moved in silence, enduring like someone performing heavy work that requires total concentration. The roll of rattan was gradually let out as the kite rose to its full height, finding stability where the wind blew in wide streams above the confused currents that imperilled it close to the ground. It inclined to one side as though it despised the earth, and to another as though it saluted it. Then, standing calmly upright in the sky, the kite played the brass flutes that were fixed to its wings:

This is the sound of the kite's flute
Does anyone know what it sings?
A fine thread alone ties the kite to the earth
A thread that can snap any time.
Yet it dares to soar high and free
For it is only a kite
That can feel the incredible lightness of life
Without harming a soul
Floating in the blue
Playing tiny flutes
That make us look up into the sky.

All suffering and even honours
You leave far beneath you now
O kite sing your song
For your own pleasure
Because destiny has already decided:
That your thread will eventually break.

The kite stabilized itself after some final oscillations. The rattan cord trailed in the sky, pushed out like a bow in the wind. Lam's father went up on to the dike and, moving along it, led the kite back to the village with the rattan cord in his hand. As the sky overflowed with the sound of the flutes, he just plodded along, head down, like somebody leading a buffalo back from the fields. I gazed in admiration at the wet muddy body of Lam's father, imagining that, while flying the kite, he had covered 9 or 10 kilometres.

At the head of the village, Lam's father tethered the end of the thick rattan cord to a bamboo stake that had been driven into the ground for that purpose. Only then did he look up into the sky with contentment, to watch the kite hovering silently above the earth. A few minutes later, he left the kite tethered to the stake and went down to the river. He stripped off, tied his shorts around his neck and, holding his genitals in one hand, waded into the water. He dived beneath the surface, and one breath took him to mid-stream where his head bobbed up again. He stopped there for a moment during which I was sure he looked up at the kite again, then cried out something I could not hear. He dived again and disappeared from view. The surface of the river was now fading into the shadows that spread across the landscape.

I went back alone along an unknown path to the hamlet. It was twilight. The world filled me with a gentle, but mysterious feeling. On either side of the path, the trees suspended their foliage in blurred masses above my head. I was adrift in time and space. Images of the city in which I lived, even the beloved faces of my parents, had been erased from my mind. It was the same for the train journey which had brought Lam and me from the city that morning. And I had completely forgotten about the kite.

Back at the house, Lam's mother was winnowing rice. His grandmother was lying in a hammock, singing a lullaby for little Tien. Lam's younger sister, Khanh, was asleep on a bamboo bed. His father occupied a low stool.

'Lam wanted to take you prawning, but he couldn't wait any longer,' his mother said to me, as I entered the house. Hien, who was grinding some rice down in the shed, called out: 'Hieu, if you're not busy, come down and give me a hand.' I went into the dark shed which was illuminated only by the wick of a tiny oil lamp. To grind the rice, Hien was operating a heavy horizontal wooden beam about 2.5 metres long. By pumping one end of the beam with her foot, Hien moved it up and down around an axle, so that the steel-tipped pestle, that was fixed to the other end of the beam, rhythmically pounded the rice in the mortar. 'Have you ever ground rice before Hieu?' she asked. 'No.' 'Get up here,' she directed. 'Hang on to the rope.' I put my foot on to the beam in front of her and picked up the rhythm. 'So grinding rice is as easy as this, is it?' I remarked confidently. 'How old are you, Hieu?' smiled Hien. 'Seventeen, the same age as Lam.' 'I'm three years older than you,' she sighed. 'That makes me old already. Women only have one spring. I'm afraid that.... Hieu, change places with me. What man stands in front of a woman, even when he's grinding rice?' But before we could change places, my body suddenly contracted with excitement at the smell of her sweat and the soft supple sensation of her breasts pushing into my back.

'It's very lonely in the country,' murmured Hien. 'I've only been to Hanoi once. I wasn't married then. I had a terrific time, but it scared me too. Hanoi people all looked wicked to me. One day, at a bus-stop, there was a man with a wispy moustache wearing dark glasses. He was old enough to be my father. "Hey there, my dear," he leered, 'how about coming with me?" I was horrified: "Oh no!" I said, "How could you ask such a thing?" He just laughed and said: "Sorry, my dear, I mistook you for a tart." I didn't know what a tart was. But a few minutes later when Tan— that's my husband—came by the bus-stop, the other fellow had taken off. This was the first time I met Tan, and when I told him the story he looked dark and said: "City louts, they're guttersnipes, the lot of them." I don't know if what he said was true, but city people are good talkers. They'll say "Sorry, my dear" for nothing.'

Hien went on: 'In the country, boredom is the worst thing. I don't mind the work. But I often get so bored that it shrivels me up. When Tan joined the army, I was so depressed that I contemplated suicide. I lay down in a corn field on a bull ants' nest. I was sure the bull ants would bite me to death. But they didn't. Did they feel sorry for me, do you think? They probably thought that I was too young to die, that it'd be a waste.' Hien laughed. I was numb. I thought of my father: he had a wispy moustache and wore dark glasses. And my mother: if she lay on an ants' nest, she would surely die; she is so restless that the bull ants could not ignore her.

Hien said: 'Of course, we also have our happy times in the country. It's good when the theatrical companies come around. I remember a performance of *Tran Si My's Neglect*. I brought along a pocketful of roasted grass hoppers. They were very tasty. I went with my friends Luoc and Thu, and the three of us ate them while we watched the play. Tran Si My was a heartless man who completely neglected his wife when he became a mandarin. It was good luck that life still had Bao Cong in store for her. What an unnatural life she would have had without him, wouldn't she? It would have been a life of injustice and despair.' Hien stopped for a moment and then burst out laughing: 'There were some young fellows from Due Dong standing right behind us. One of them came and pressed himself up against Luoc's bottom. Luoc said: "What are you doing?" Without batting an eyelid, the dirty fellow said calmly: "I'm the director of a co-operative." Luoc scolded him: "Stop it!" she said. The fellow said: "I'll keep doing it as long as the people have confidence in me." Everyone around burst out laughing. Luoc ran out with the back of her pants wet. She was so scared this would make her pregnant that as soon as she got home she threw her pants into the pond. That's the story of *Tran Si My's Neglect!*'

Hien said: 'Hieu stop breathing so hard. Take a deep breath.... Now breathe slowly. You breathe like the fat major who trains in the village. His name is Ba, he's retired. Every morning he puts on a pair of shorts and runs around the village yelling: "1, 2, 3, 4.... Fitness!" One time, I was on my way to do some transplanting with Thu. It was early, around four in the morning, and we saw Mr Ba running along the road. The cord in his shorts had broken, and he was running along holding them up with his hands. Thu called out to him: "Hey, Pop, you're already sixty, what are you getting fit for?" Mr Ba replied, "I've got to be fit to take care of the family. You girls don't know my wife's just turned forty, do you?" Anyway, he's a good man. He's always willing to help.... It's said that he was not retired because of his age, but because he's not too bright. Apparently, the government only takes clever young people with an education these days.'

Hien continued: 'Why do women have to get married? Like me here, my husband is always away, so having a husband is the same as not having one. Hieu, would you say that it was good to leave your husband?' 'No,' I answered. 'That's right,' said Hien, ' "a piece of bamboo left to drift on the river will either be cracked or broken. A girl who scorns marriage will have one defect if she doesn't have another." ' 'What does all that mean, Hien?' I asked. 'It means that women are worth nothing. But there are many men who aren't worth much either. It's very dangerous for a woman to marry a man who is poor and untalented, but full of noble ideas. A man like that can crush a woman so easily.' 'Why do you think that, Hien?' I asked her. 'Oh, they are not all my ideas,' she replied. 'I've been listening to Mr Trieu. He takes the adult night classes in culture. He says women don't need noble ideas. They need understanding and caresses and lots of money. That's love. Noble ideas are best left to politicians, for politics is a very dirty business without them.'

I was feeling exhausted. It was as though I had lost track of the time since I last slept. The next morning it felt strange to wake up in the absolute silence of an empty house. No one was there. I went out and washed my face and looked around. Down in the shed, a few empty paddy baskets were stacked up against the mortar. The kite had been tossed to one side with a torn wing—I could neither see its flutes nor its rattan cord. In the kitchen there was a plate of boiled sweet potatoes and eggplant that I felt sure had been left for me. After eating the potato and eggplant, I went and sat down in the house. I noticed that the painting of the Lords of Happiness, Good Fortune, and Longevity was a water-colour print inscribed with Chinese characters. I liked the Lord of Good Fortune best with his black beard, chubby cheeks, and stout healthy body. His eyes seemed to speak: 'I understand completely, be calm, we are all in accord, do not try to deceive me.'

About ten o'clock, Lam's grandmother came back to the

house with Khanh and Tien. 'The three of us have been to the pagoda,' said the old woman. 'The old monk gave us some consecrated rice cakes. Khanh, give one to Hieu to taste so he'll know what they're like.' 'You eat it yourself, Grandmother, I have just eaten some sweet potatoes,' I said. 'No no, I won't eat it. I have been eating for a long time. If you're still a glutton at eighty, it makes it very hard to die. These last four years, I haven't dared to eat anything nutritious, but I still haven't been able to die.'

The old woman took a long breath: 'If you live too long, you go crazy, my boy. Why do I hate old age so much? Each morning I go to the pagoda and pray to the Buddha Nhu Lai to let me die, but he is still shaking his head. He hasn't accepted me yet. But I suppose it has all been my own doing. I have toiled all my life, but if I had not, if I had wasted my life when I was young, then maybe I would not be where I am now. In the village, the girls of my generation who behaved shamelessly in their youth are all gone now. The merciful Buddha let them go early. They didn't have to wait for the age of wisdom: they lived happily and died happily. As for me, I've had a reputation for being faithful and virtuous all my life, and I don't know if it's done anyone any good. I only know that if you live too long all you do is annoy your children and grandchildren.'

I smiled sorrowfully and said: 'Don't talk like that, Grandmother.' She shook her head: 'You are still very young, you'll see when you are eighty. Buddha gives everyone a little store of wealth; everyone's the same; each gets his due. Health and virtue are riches, and if you have them, you must know how to expend them. If you hoard them, they become malevolent. Over at Due Dong, there was a man who hoarded gold in his house: his wife went mad, his children were imbeciles, and none of his descendants lived until they were thirty.'

Lam and his father returned after some ploughing. 'It's already midday, hasn't anyone cooked lunch yet?' asked Lam's father. 'I'm cooking', called Khanh from the kitchen. Lam's father came into the house, poured some tea, and offered me some. 'So you haven't been anywhere?' he said. 'If you sit around listening to Grandmother's stories, you'll go crazy.' 'That's right, I'm stupid,' said Grandmother Lam. 'Not stupid, but venomous,' said Lam's father. 'A cruel heart is something to be afraid of, but there's nothing to fear from a sharp tongue,' she replied. 'He's young and as untroubled as a well of clear water. So why disturb him by releasing a bag full of river serpents into it,' said Lam's father. The old woman thought for a moment and said slightly chastened: 'Ah, don't listen to me, my boy. I am eight parts devil, one part wraith, one part human. Listen to the tiny part that pleases you and ignore the rest.'

When lunch was over, the teacher, Mr Trieu, came over for a visit. He was a thin, languid-looking man of about thirty, and I was vaguely aware of Hien's body tensing in his calm gaze. 'You've come for a stay in the country, how do you like it?' he asked me. 'I like it very much.' Mr Trieu laughed: 'I suppose that was a stupid question,' he said. 'You are a guest and, if you said you didn't like it, Uncle Ba Dinh would tell you to get lost.' 'I wouldn't do that,' said Lam's father. 'Uncle Ba Dinh, your guest is as bashful as a girl. I see he looks intelligent, but perhaps prone to misfortune too. I hope he has no plans to become a scholar. Listen to me, young man: when you grow up make sure you don't take the path of literature. You'll be cut to pieces and covered by insults. Do nothing to expose the stupidity of the educated. Take me, I know well how damaging their stupidity can be: they are reactionary, dangerous, devious. The stupidity of the educated is ten thousand times more nauseating than that of ordinary people.' 'Why is that?' I asked. 'Because they are hypocrites. They dissimulate in the name of conscience, morality, aesthetics, social order, even in the name of the people! That's what a literary education leads to.'

Trieu paused and said to Hien: 'The night lectures are over now. You can go up to the eighth grade. You got eight points for your maths paper and three for literature, but I put it up to five.' Hien blushed: 'I'm very stupid at literature.' 'That does not matter,' said Trieu. 'What our people are good at is fighting. I've never thought our literature is worth much. It lacks strong beliefs and beauty.' After he had told Hien her results, Trieu departed. 'He's clever, isn't he?' I commented. 'He's a good fellow,' said Lam's father. 'All the children in the village study with him. In my generation, we all studied with his grandfather, Mr Dat.'

All of a sudden, the sky darkened. Within seconds it began to rain so heavily that the courtyard was soon flooded. 'Look at the flying fish there! The flying fish!' cried Khanh, who darted straight out into the courtyard to try and catch one. I braved the rain and went out after her. 'Hien,' she called, 'get the fish-trap for me.' Hien, who was standing on the veranda, looked up at the sky, and then said to Lam's father: 'The weather's changed. Let's get the fish net down to the river.' Khanh shouted: 'Let's go to the river! Let's go to the river!'

While Lam's father put the net over his shoulder, I picked up the fish-trap. Hien grabbed a bamboo basket, Khanh took hold of a crab pot, and we all went down to the river. The rain came down in torrents, as thousands of fish bobbed up and down in the swollen stream, breaking the surface of the water. Hien said: 'Look over there, Father, can you see all those fish? And look at the shrimps!' Lam's father waded into the river until he was waist deep and cast the net. Hien, Khanh, and I pulled it in, pouring the fish out on to the sand. Lam's father cast the net again and again, each time with success. In the catch were some very fat slimy sheatfish, which have no scales.

With the rain still falling heavily, I began to feel the cold. Hien and Khanh must have felt it too, for their teeth were now chattering along with mine. We were tired by our exertions, but did not notice it in all the excitement and continued to have a good time.

Eventually, Lam's father cast the net twice without catching more fish. He let the net droop and said to us: 'I'll go back ahead of you. I have to go and drain the water off the rice seedlings or they will be ruined. You come back when you are ready.' Hien filled the bamboo basket with fish and said to Khanh: 'Come down and have a wash.' The two of them waded into the water with their clothes on. I hesitated for a moment before going in after them. The water was very warm. I did not go out very far into the river, because swimming was new to me. Hien said: 'Hieu's not a good swimmer!'

We swam for about ten minutes, then got out of the water. Hien and Khanh stood near me on the bank with their wet clothes clinging tightly to their bodies. Their curves were so beautiful that I could not take my eyes off them. My blood pounded in a quickening pulse that I had never felt before. Hien called out: 'Come and give me a hand, Hieu'. Our eyes crossed. I caught a fleeting glimpse of some cruel irony at the corners of her cheerful smile. I went to the basket and bent over to pick it up, when she casually brushed her thigh against my body. This paralysed me. Hien looked deeply into my eyes, then blushed. I gulped, my legs gave way, and I collapsed on to the sand. Hien put her hand on my head. Pale with embarrassment, she mumbled something, before she ran off to catch up with Khanh who had gone ahead with the fish-trap. In the distance, I could hear their tinkling laughter.

I rolled around panting on the stretch of wet sand, accidentally overturning the basket. As a result, I found myself face down with a mouth full of sand in a slithering mass of fish and prawns. I don't know if I swallowed the sand. But flooded with feelings of joy and fear, I knew that I had become an adult.

The rain had stopped. However, the sky was still overcast as I returned to the house. When she saw the fish I had regathered in the basket, Lam's mother said: 'With a bit of luck, I'll catch the afternoon market. I'll take them down and sell them.' She put a few of the largest fish aside, gave Khanh some instructions, and hurried off with the basket. Equipped with a knife and chopping board, Khanh went out to the pond to clean the fish. I felt so sleepy that I went and lay down on the bed.

After I had dozed off for some time, I was woken by the sound of giggling in the courtyard. Khanh and Tien sat on the edge of the veranda playing a game of pick-up-sticks. Khanh dropped a bundle of bamboo sticks on the ground, then picked them up as she tossed a pebble into the air. Tien knelt down beside her, trying to imitate the song she sang in a high-pitched voice: 'Toss toss once: one pair. Toss toss, two potatoes: two pairs. Toss toss, three potatoes: three pairs. Toss toss, four: four pairs. Toss toss, five: five pairs. Change hands. . . .'

Grandmother Lam sat on the edge of the bed with tears rolling down her wizened cheeks. Khanh's voice still sounded shrilly: 'On entering the village, I ask for meat; on leaving, I ask for rice. I cross the river going, I cross it coming back. I plant a cabbage tree. The river boats go by. One boat, two boats. . . .'

I left the house and wandered down the path. Without warning, the sky lit up in a strangely beautiful creamy glow. Everything around me stood out with incredible clarity in one dazzling dreamlike colour. Every object, every plant was suffused in the glow, including the hibiscus bushes whose dark red flowers faded into the pink of peoples' lips beneath their lustrous coats of cream. Another world had opened up in terrifying detail before my eyes. Its unreal beauty took my breath away.

Soon, the sky lost its momentary radiance. The world returned to its former colours which I recognized with a shudder. High up in the sky, some egrets flew overhead making alarming, raucous cries. Some rain drops, still hanging on a leaf, fell and struck my body. I continued along the narrow path covered with fallen leaves, and circled around the village for a while because I had lost my way. A few children ran wildly across my path. Some people who had lost a chicken directed a coarse stream of curses at their neighbours' house. I wandered around and went up to the edge of the dike. A long way off on the river, a brown sail moved upstream with slow unruffled poise.

At the dike, I came across Trieu reading a book. Near where he was sitting, I noticed a clump of purple flowers with slightly open petals that faintly suggested human lips. I plucked one of these flowers and held it up to my nose: it gave off a lush scent. Trieu laughed: 'Do you know what kind of flower it is?' I shook my head. 'It is a very strange flower,' he said. 'It looks like a smiling mouth. However, if some foolish fly falls into it, it snaps its petals shut. What is unusual about it is that nothing happens if it's left alone; but as soon as it is touched, it gives off its overpowering scent.

We call it the "harlot's herb". It's exactly the same with women who are attractive as long as no one touches them. But as soon as a man lays a hand on them, he loses everything before he knows what has happened: first his money, then his soul, his family, his profession.' 'Are you married, Mr Trieu?' I laughed. He replied drolly: 'Other people's wives are always too desirable, and I am too correct. That's the problem!'

Trieu fell back on to the patch of green grass. 'Lie down here,' he said. 'Do you feel superior to country people because you live in the city?' 'No,' I said. 'Mm, don't despise them,' he went on. 'All city people and the educated élite carry a heavy burden of guilt when it comes to the villages. We crush them with our material demands. With our pork stew of science and education, we have a conception of civilization and an administrative superstructure that is designed to squeeze the villages.... So you understand? My heart bleeds. I always say that "My mother is a peasant and I am a child of the country."' Trieu was silent for a moment. Then he sat up and said in a disappointed tone: 'You'll never be able to understand the meaning of what I've said to you.' 'Don't you have confidence in me?' I asked. 'It's not that,' he said. 'It's because you're young. The fault lies in nature, not in you.'

At this point, an ant bit me. As I sat up, I observed a mass of black ants swarming around a dead dragon-fly at my feet. 'So many ants!' I remarked. 'That's right,' said Trieu, 'That's a likeness of our people: multitudes moving in mindless circles, with most unable to make a living. Put the dragon-fly in another spot and see what happens.' I did what he said. 'Can you see the ants teeming again in masses around there?' he asked. 'Yes,' I said. Trieu went on: 'The masses are as gullible and as light-headed as that. They chase material gain, but they do not realize that therein lies the absurdity of their lives. They are born, are active, seek a living, and are swept in perpetuity from one situation to another, without any control over the direction of their lives. Only when the masses understand the futility of their dreams, only when they realize that no one will give them an easy life for nothing, will they perceive that they are plied with nothing but empty promises or see that what they do receive is little more than false hope against need. All the people's gains must be created by the force of their own labour. They need to seek something beyond empty gains that gives value to their lives: this is the power to determine their own destinies which, in sum, is freedom.'

Silence settled around us for a few moments before Trieu said: 'Don't listen to me. My ideas are shallow and mistaken. My mother is a peasant, and I am a child of the country. . . . ' I looked at him with a heavy heart, and felt so moved that I had to push my face down into the grass so that he could not see me crying.

Trieu stood up to go down to the edge of the dike, when a loud bellowing came from the fields. An enraged buffalo charged in our direction. At exactly the moment I became aware of this, I heard the sound of someone calling: 'Hieu, it's time for dinner!' I looked around to see little Tien standing at the foot of the dike. Drawn by the sound of Tien's voice, the buffalo was now charging straight towards him. Before I could overcome my panic, I saw Trieu jump in front of Tien. All I heard was the sound of Tien's blood-curdling scream, as the buffalo charged into Trieu's body with terrifying force. I saw the buffalo lift Trieu on its horns and toss him into the air.

Trieu died before my eyes. His head fell to one side, while his mouth gushed blood and his entrails hung from his disembowelled body. Near by, the buffalo calmly nibbled the grass. Little Tien, whom Trieu had pushed into a ditch at the side of the rice field, crawled out gingerly, with his face a bluish leaden colour.

Within no time at all, people from the hamlet had begun to arrive. Among these people a few were armed, including one militiaman who unslung his rifle and emptied a full magazine into the animal's head. By now a large crowd had rushed out of the hamlet. Grandmother Lam held little Tien's hand, while the two cried and bowed low before the body of Trieu. Lam's mother and father also cried as they knelt down in the field to bow repeatedly before it too. After their deliberations, the hamlet elders finally decided that Trieu's body should be taken to the foot of the banyan tree at the end of the village. This ancient tree, which was over 900 years old, had spread its branches so widely that it looked like a rice tray when viewed from afar, and its trunk was so big that it took four people to link arms around its circumference.

Night had fallen. The moon glistened in the sky like a pool of silver suspended in the spray of a million stars. As I looked up in awesome wonder, I was as overwhelmed as I had been in the creamy radiance of the afternoon sky. Again, the limitless mystery of the universe had made me acutely aware of the meaninglessness of my own life and death.

Trieu's coffin was made at the foot of the banyan tree. Lam and a number of youths from the hamlet brought incense and set up an altar. A photograph, an incense burner, a plate of fruit, betel leaves, and areca nuts were placed on it. Everyone in the village had gathered around the foot of the tree. Someone had brought a mat with a floral print and spread it out on the ground for the old men and women to sit and prepare their betel quids. Militiamen mounted guard with their rifles. The sad solemn atmosphere of the gathering was loaded with the anxiety of everyone who was a part of it.

As Trieu's body was placed in the coffin at midnight, flaming torches illuminated the area. Everyone wore funeral turbans. Lam's mother gave me one too, which I guessed had been torn from an old curtain because of the black needle marks it bore. While the drums and trumpets sounded, the women and children cried throughout. I also cried.

With the body in the coffin, Lam's father and some youths went back to the house to slaughter a pig and cook some glutinous rice. By daylight the funeral feast was ready.

Trieu's funeral took place at eight in the morning when the fields were soaked in sunlight. The old men and women and others from the hamlet assembled around the coffin. In front of it, Trieu's pupils stood in ranks. Mr Mieu, the school principal, read the funeral oration, and all the while his body trembled. As I listened, I was surprised to learn that Trieu was not from this village. His parents lived in Hanoi where his father was a government minister and his mother had come from a well-known family of intellectuals. Trieu had lived alone in the village for nine years and never visited his family in the city. People said that his family had disowned him, because he was only an ordinary primary schoolteacher.

Trieu was buried in the village cemetery. A single wreath of white flowers was placed on the grave. I would attend many more funerals in the future, but I already knew that this one had made such a deep impression on me that it would not fade.

That afternoon no one left the house to go to work, except Lam, who took the buffalo out to harrow the fields. His mother prepared a rice offering for Trieu's soul. Hien, who still wore her funeral turban, cried as she plucked a chicken. Lam's mother said to her: 'Hien, take off that turban. If our sorrow is sincere, it is enough to keep it in our hearts. People will look askance if they see you wearing it while your husband is away.' Hien removed the turban and cried: 'Dear Teacher, you were wise in life and are sacred in death, please continue to protect and care for my family.' Grandmother Lam said: 'The teacher gave his life for little Tien. Even though he was a stranger, he's suddenly become a saint in this house. Anyway, he's worthy of our esteem.' Mr Mieu was sitting down drinking tea with Lam's father. 'Trieu was a grandchild of the old teacher Dat,' said Mr Mieu. 'Dat was from Ninh Xa where he had a foot in the scholars' group that fought the French all those years ago. He came from a line that has produced very many heroes.' 'What a miserable lot the girls in this village are,' Grandmother Lam piped up. 'It seems that not one of them loved the teacher. It's a waste for someone like that to die without leaving anyone to carry on the family line, don't you think?' 'I once heard he had an interest in Thu, but she spurned him as a cold philosopher,' said Hien. 'The silly wench!' cried Grandmother Lam. 'I'll tell her what I think of her when she next comes here. All you girls are interested in these days is making up your faces and falling into the arms of the first lady-killer that comes along.' Mr Mieu added: 'Our country's heroes are dying out because all the beautiful girls fall for light-headed lady-killers and scoffers. It's a great pity.' 'I'm not sure I like philosophy myself,' interposed Lam's father. 'But our people have to have a philosophy of death. There are so many accidental deaths in our country it's frightening,' said Mr Mieu. 'Everyone lives as though he hasn't got time. That was Trieu's fate.'

Late in the afternoon after the funeral feast was over, a Madame Hop from the next hamlet came by Lam's house with a number of women from the transplanting team. Madame Hop yelled from the gate: 'Hey, Mr Ba Dinh, come out and take a look at some of your son's handiwork.

His ploughing is sloppy, his harrowing is worse: he's uprooted some of our rice seedlings. Look at these, you'll have to replace them.' Lam ran from the house with a scarlet face. 'Can't you replant the seedlings?' asked Lam's father. 'If we could replant them, we wouldn't be here complaining,' answered Madame Hop. 'I am sorry,' said Lam, 'all I could think of was getting back to the funeral feast.' Lam's father shouted: 'Get down here! Three lashes will give you something to think about. Madame Hop, let me send my son out with the harrows to repair the damage for you.' Lam's father took down a rattan switch from the roof of the house, while his son lay face down in the court-yard. Everyone gathered around to try to mollify Lam's father. 'Get out of my way, you women, and let me teach this boy a lesson,' he scowled. 'He must remember his care-less work! He's got to go out into the world to make a living. How's he going to do that if he's in the habit of cheating like that?' Lam's mother pulled at her husband's arm: 'Not too hard now, just give him a gentle reminder.'

Lam's father raised the switch into the air and informed his son: 'Three lashes. Two to remind you to work carefully. One to remind you that you are the son of old Ba Dinh who doesn't like having people come to insult him.' Lam's bottom bounced up three times as the switch went up in the air and came down on its target. 'You brute!' said Lam's mother, pulling the switch from her husband's hand. Lam then crawled painfully to his feet and clasped his hands saying: 'Forgive me, Father.' With this, Lam's father walked down towards the kitchen with his head down. He untied the buffalo, put the harrows over his shoulder, and went out through the gate.

At nightfall, Khanh came running into the house. 'Brother Lam,' she called out, 'there is a letter for Hieu.' I was surprised to find that it was a letter from my father. It read:

Dear Son,

I was extremely angry to learn that your mother took advantage of my absence to allow you to go to the country. Let me tell you, you fool, that our stamping ground is the city. That is where your future lies. It is a great mistake for intellectuals to associate with peasants.

Listen to me, my boy, and come home immediately. Your mother and I will welcome you with open arms like a naive, an unbelievably naive boy....

Your Father

I was stunned. I gave Lam the letter to read. He said: 'Well, Hieu, you'll have to go home. Your father won't whip you like mine whipped me; with a letter like that, he'll kill you. There is a train at five tomorrow morning.'

Early the next morning Hien got up to cook some glutinous rice, which she wrapped in banana leaves and put in my bag. 'Can you get to the station by yourself?' asked Lam. I nodded. Everyone in the house seemed busy, without showing any interest in me. I knew I had no right to expect the slightest attention, and certainly no affection from any of them: Lam's grandmother, father, mother, Hien, Khanh, or little Tien.

It was still dark when I left the village. The fields were covered in a heavy frost. I asked myself why my father thought I was so naive:

Naivety is a thing of the heart
I am naive
You are naive, big sister
You are naive, big brother

And you too, little sister
You are extremely naive
'We are all naive in this life
I was naive to believe my father
I was naive to believe my brothers and sisters
And you too, little sister
You are extremely naive
Your heart is pure
Your lips are pure
Your eyes are intense
Your belief has no foundation,
No verification, no conditions
And if I am a demon
You big brother, are you a demon?
You big sister, are you a demon too?
Naivety is a thing of the heart
Does it not let us spread our wings
So that we can fly to heaven?

I kept walking for a long time. I made my way across the fields and crossed the river, all the while with the sun on my face.

I still remember it.... I was seventeen that year. Nhai Hamlet, Thach Dao Village, N Province.

Run River Run

THE river running past Coc Jetty pushes out around a sandy promontory in an arc to the west. The ferry-stop is located at the foot of a solitary kapok tree which stands at the head of a hamlet. When the kapok tree flowers, its canopy is covered by blooms that are so red they are strangely disturbing. Like a spearhead in mid-stream, the river's current carves a channel through the drift, creating waves that pulse in its wake. The ferry-stop is quiet; very few people pass by it. In winter, black magpies with yellow legs perch on the steel hand-rail that extends out along the jetty from the base of the kapok tree. With their heads slanted down over the stream of running water, the magpies grip the steel, squawking. Evening falls, the sound of a church bell reaches Coc Jetty and spreads over the moving surface of the river's endless flow. The river seems startled for an instant, then relaxes in its silent drift. It is like a wise man who understands some noisy activity going on around him, but who, lost in thought, neither needs nor wants to know anything about it.

The river and that ferry-stop are bound up with my early years. The ferry-stop was about 500 metres from my house, and, after school, I would wander down and play there from time to time.

Usually, I liked the herring season best. I was fascinated by the slap of the waves and the knocking sounds which the fishermen made on the sides of their basket-boats as they chased the fish at night. Dim starlight swept down across the surface of the water in beautiful silver streaks. A few dozen basket-boats drifted in the perfect calm. The sound of a few short coughs, the sharp wet gurgle of tobacco smoke being drawn through a water-pipe, the murmur of prayers from a bible meeting: all of these were infinitely pleasing to my ear. Towards morning, a ribbon of mist unfurled on the river, blurring the boundaries between the jetty and the bank, the surface of the water and the sky. The bottoms of the boats were full of silvery, white herrings. The acrid smell of smoke and the fatty fragrance of roasted fish mingled in the clean morning air. All these sights and sensations were wonderful to me.

Even more wonderful was the credulous folk tale about the black buffaloes in this stretch of the river. People who went fishing at night were convinced they had seen them. The buffaloes usually appear at midnight and rise to the surface from the bottom of the river. Their bodies glisten, their horns stand high, their snouts puff plumes of hot breath, and they charge across the surface of the water foaming at the mouth. This foam is like spawn, and it is said that anyone who is lucky enough to get some of it will be endowed with extraordinary powers which include being able to swim underwater like a fish.

All of this magic had the power to carry me away in my childhood. I wanted to see the buffaloes with all my heart, and, who knows, perhaps I could have enjoyed that marvellous sight which I went looking for often enough. As soon as night fell, I would leave the house, ignoring my books and my mother's advice. I would go down to the ferry-stop and beg the fishermen to let me help them, until one of them took pity on me and allowed me to get into his boat.

'I'll just take you past Coc Jetty, all right!' my brave boat owner bargained one night. 'You're as dumb as a dog; in this cold you should be at home snuggled up in bed. What do you want to catch herrings for?'

'He wants to start a co-operative when he grows up,' laughed some dark fat figure from a boat near by. 'Good Lord! Our brat is so expert at night fishing, there'll only be fish bones left for us to eat.'

'Throw him into the river for Ha Ba, the god of the waters,' some fellow said threateningly, as his boat glided by and he gave me a painful blow in the ribs with his paddle.

'If you let him mess up our fishing all night, you'll see what happens to you!' growled an old man with one eye, who raised his paddle without any trace of a jest.

'All right, out you get!,' my boat owner said, a little uneasily. 'Old Thinh doesn't joke!'

'Please, Mister,' I moaned, 'you said you'd take me past Coc Jetty.'

'Which jetty?' Both irritated and embarrassed, my boat owner turned the boat towards the shore. 'You've just got into the boat, and the water is flowing in. By the end of Coc Jetty, I'll go to the bottom of the river with Ha Ba, won't I?'

I got out of the boat and watched it move off with tears welling up in my eyes. Fish swam around my legs, and I could feel their soft greasy fins brushing my feet.

There was one occasion when the dark fat fellow let me sit in his boat. His name was Tao. He had a pair of glassy eyes like those of a fish, and his left cheek had been permanently disfigured by a scar the size of the palm of my hand. He spoke to me in a soft slippery voice.

'I'll let you get into my boat, but you must do whatever I tell you,' he said. 'When I was your age, I went fishing at night like you. Now, I'll cast the net, then pull it in hard.'

A light rain chilled the night. The net felt as heavy as chains. 'This time I think I've got a big catch,' said Tao. 'When I pull the net into the boat, you'll know if we've caught anything or not.'

What came up in the net was a human head. It was bloated like an overripe persimmon. Its hair hung down in strands tangled with algae as long as earthworms. Its nostrils were stained with blood. I put my hand into its jaws, and dropping straight out of the gums were teeth with three pronged roots as long as finger joints. These were sticky with fatty gum tissue. The eyes in the head glared rudely with the pupils popping slowly out at me, as if the head belonged to someone who was being pumped up with air.

I was terrified. Without anyone in control of it, the boat began to twirl around in the small eddies in the current. Tao suddenly yelled: 'Is that the way you row a boat? Scared out of your pants, are you?' He took hold of my chest with fingers like plump bananas. 'Off this boat immediately, please, Sir! If I pull in another head with you in the boat, it will be the end of me!'

I sobbed bitterly and begged him to let me stay. Our boat was in the middle of the river. The kapok tree at the ferry-stop was so far away, it looked like a tiny hand with many troubled fingers gesticulating at the sky.

'Jump out!' Tao yelled fiercely, baring his teeth. 'If you don't jump, I'll wrap this paddle around your head!'

I slipped down into the stream of water and swam silently in the direction of the kapok tree. Tao turned his boat upstream, and the sound of his laughter rippled menacingly across the surface of the water. 'Swim carefully there. Just in front of you, that's the spot where I pulled up the head!'

I clenched my teeth tightly to stop myself from crying. My heart missed a beat. The current was running fast. It frightened me into the realization that it always runs fast, and that I would have to make a big effort to reach the bank.

There was another time I spent a whole night fishing for herrings. On that occasion I was in Thinh's boat. This one-eyed old man was famous for his horrifying exploits. When he was young, he joined the French army. His wife had two children with white skin, blue eyes, and long noses. He killed a French captain and took his wife back. In town, he was certainly involved in various burglaries, for, every now and then, the local committee sent him to prison for a few days. He opened a dumpling soup shop, and people said he used rat meat in the dumplings. It was also said that the meat came from rats he had poisoned with arsenic. A bowl of these dumplings had killed a dog. Then, the dog killed someone who ate it. The shop was open for a few weeks before the old man piled up some straw inside it and burnt it down. There were people who said that when the flames leapt into the air, a rat as fat as a calf muscle shot out of the inferno, sniggering. This was the terrible old man who agreed to take me along with him. When I climbed into the boat, I was trembling like a bird. But my fascination for the wonderful mysteries of the river overcame my fear. I began to paddle the boat and did my best to carry out old Thinh's orders.

The old man told me to steer the boat along the side of the river where the bank had been eroded. We were about half a kilometre from the other boats. I watched how the old man controlled the boat and realized that he was a really skilled hand on the river. He knew all the spots where the boat should stop. Often, he also lay down half asleep and let me take charge. Around midnight he suddenly woke up, gabbling like a magpie.

'Fishing is the oldest profession', the old man said to me. 'In the Bible, Simon, who was called Peter, and his brothers were fishermen. When Jesus first saw them as he walked along the shore of Lake Galilee, they were casting their nets. Jesus said, "Follow me, and I will teach you to catch men."' Old Thinh hissed through a puff of tobacco smoke and continued sadly. 'The other day up in town, the public security police asked me: "What is your profession?" I said I was a fisherman. They rolled around laughing. "You catch people in nets. That's the truth!" Good heavens! It turns out I'm the same as Saint Simon.'

Old Thinh continued: 'Of all the professions, a burglar's is the most leisurely. . . . Once, when it was raining, some sly layabouts in the village came and said to me: "Thinh, you old rogue, it would be good if we had some dog meat for dinner!" I said, "When you come to my noble house you always get what you want." That's all I said, but was still worried I'd lose my balls with them around. Suddenly, I remembered that dogs were killed in the afternoon at the Canton Chief's house. So, I put on my shirt and went there. I went up to the kitchen where the smell of a pork and dog meat stew made me feel good. I looked into the house and saw a group playing cards. I went casually into the kitchen and asked the cooks, "Is the dog meat cooked yet? The old people are waiting for it up there. . . . Let me take a bowl for some fellows to eat at the back, then I'll carry the pot up to the house." I did what I said. The dim louts stuck their heads into the bowl of meat, and I took off with the pot!'

The old man laughed loudly, making my heart heave with a sharp pain. The pale beams of a crescent moon dimly illuminated the sandy promontory. The wind blew in gentle gusts. There were some night birds that flew past making sorrowful cries. It seemed as though the surface of the river was so wide that the river had no banks. From the direction of the kapok tree, the pink rays of dawn began to glimmer.

I asked old Thinh a question: 'Uncle, is the story about the black buffaloes true?' The old knave laughed and leaned over the helm with light twinkling in his one eye. 'I've been fishing along this stretch of the river for sixty years. I belong to the currents. The story of the black buffaloes is only a fairy-tale. Believe me, the story of me killing the robber at Coc Jetty is true, the adultery is true, the gambling is true, but the story of the black buffaloes is false.'

I secretly sighed. The boat bobbed along on the stream.

A little later, our boat had drifted into the middle of the river. All the other boats were gradually gathering at one spot, and the rapid knocking sound that came across the surface of the water was very noisy. Thinh suddenly jumped up. 'A school of fish!' he said in a tone that went strangely off key.

The other boats had also detected the fish. A contest took place as the sound of fishing nets breaking the surface of the water rained down along the river. Our boat was jammed between two others so that we could not cast our net. Old Thinh grumbled and cursed. He thrust the paddle into the water, and the boat jumped forward, making me fall on my back. I intended to sit up, but the boat rolled to one side and, before I knew what was happening, it threw me into the river. I panicked as I gulped and choked on the water. I called out for help until I lost my voice. My legs were stiff and racked with sharp pains. I sank beneath the surface, and I remembered in terror that the fishermen had a rule not to recover anyone who had drowned. As I lost consciousness, I was vaguely aware of an inner voice that seemed to be saying to me: 'This year, Ha Ba hasn't caught anyone yet.'

There was the sound of a woman screaming, and I passed out with the sky crashing down on me. . . .

When I woke up, I was lying on a ferry-boat. A woman wearing a scarf wrapped around her face was sitting beside me. A pair of glad black eyes looked down at me: 'So you've woken up already. Do you want a little fish soup?'

I tried to get up. My stomach was empty and painful, and my limbs trembled. I welcomed the hot bowl of fish soup, but held it unsteadily.

'Let me feed you,' the woman said sweetly. 'I thought you were dead. Your arms and legs were all stiff. Old Tao emptied half a bucket of water out of your stomach. You're very foolhardy! If you go fishing at night with that old knave Thinh, you're bound to die.'

'Did you save me?' I asked.

'Yes, I heard you crying for help.'

'These fishermen are so cruel, aren't they,' I said sadly. 'They heard me cry out but ignored me.'

'Don't reproach them,' the woman comforted me in a lilting voice. 'No one loves them. They are so hungry it makes them callous and stupid.'

These words surprised me, because nobody had ever spoken to me like that before.

That morning the sky was astonishingly beautiful. It was one of those winter days when the sun generously spreads its dazzling glory across the surface of the earth. The sky was very blue. A gust of wind blew some grains of sand on to the boat and sucked them up into a little whirlwind.

From the side of the river, there came the sound of some-one singing a very unusual song in a sad voice:

Run river run
What's the use of worrying?
The river has carried everything away
What's left for heroes?

The song hung in the air across the surface of the river. A thick mist came off the water, and a pleasant feeling came over me. It was as though I had just finished bathing and scrubbed myself clean.

That was how I got to know Tham. Her house was near Coc Jetty. It was a very poor house, and she spent all day on the ferry-boat with her scarf covering her face.

I once asked Tham about the story of the black buffaloes. 'They are real!' she said. 'They live under the water. When they come up on to the bank, they bring us strength. But to see them, and to receive their marvellous miracles you have to be a good person.'

I believed what Tham said. I had always cherished the thought of seeing those wonderful miracles.

'Human beings are very stupid,' she said to me, as we sat on the prow of the ferry, waiting for someone to hire the boat for the river crossing. 'They are as mindless as dust.'

I listened to her, watching the flowers on the kapok tree occasionally drop their deep red petals on to the stretch of wet sand below them.

I dozed off to sleep, vaguely aware of the story Tham whispered about the saints in paradise: 'Once upon a time, in Jerusalem, there was a man. . . .'

In the summer of that year my family moved to the city, far

from Coc Jetty and far from Tham. When I was leaving, Tham called me down to the ferry-boat to eat fish soup. I did not realize that that was the last bowl of herring soup I would eat in my childhood. A new life opened up for me. Herrings were sold in the city, but there they were dried and gutted.

I do not know any more how long it took me to adjust to the rhythm of city life. I gradually grew up and was caught in so many ephemeral concerns. Those nights when I went fishing for herrings and that folk tale about the black buffaloes which captivated me in my childhood had faded from my memory.

Last year, I had an unexpected opportunity to return to Coc Jetty. I was now an adult. I worked for the government, was married with a tribe of children and lived a very bourgeois life. Perhaps I had nothing to complain about in all of this. But, my return to the jetty made me painfully aware of how the dreams of my childhood had yielded to the practical demands of my life.

Coc Jetty was just the same as it was in the old days. Very few people passed by it. The lonely kapok tree still stood in the same place with its bright red flowers stirring me deeply. I stepped down to the jetty with confused feelings that are difficult to describe.

An old woman sat pensively on the ferry-boat. I stepped up close to her and asked quietly: 'Old lady, is the ferry woman, Tham, still here?'

'Tham?' The old woman was slightly surprised.

As I stood in silence, I recognized the old ferry. My childhood memories leapt back to life.

'You know Tham, Sir?' the old woman asked me in a sorrowful voice. 'No one has asked for Tham for many years. She was drowned a long time ago.'

Tears welled up in my eyes. The blurred waters of the river ran on. The ferry woman continued in a melancholy tone: 'It is wretched. I don't know how many people Tham saved in this section of the river. Then, in the end, she drowned and no one saved her.'

Down at the river, I again heard the sound of a song that was as mournful to me as ever:

Run river run
What's the use of worrying?
The river has carried everything away
What's left for heroes?

I wanted to cry out in pain. I was overwhelmed by the emptiness of my life. The black buffaloes of my youth, where were they now?

The sound of someone calling out loudly for the ferry rose over the river: 'Ferry! Ferry! Hey, ferry!'

Other Oxford Paperbacks for readers interested in South-East Asia, past and present

Titles marked with an asterisk have restricted rights.